THE NO SLEEPER TRAIN

MR. MICHAEL SQUID

VELOX BOOKS

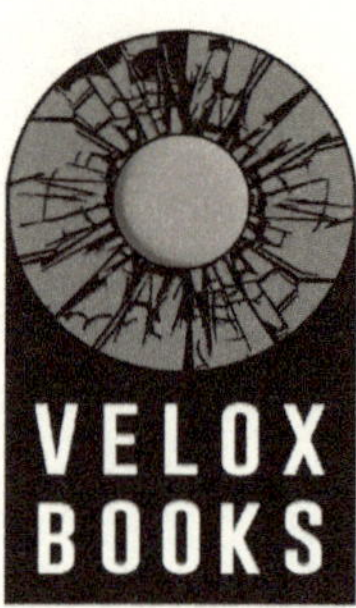

Published by arrangement with the author.

Copyright © 2025 by Michael Squid.

All rights reserved.

YOU'RE READING ANOTHER TERRIFYING COLLECTION FROM

**FOLLOW VELOX TO KEEP
THE NIGHTMARES COMING:**

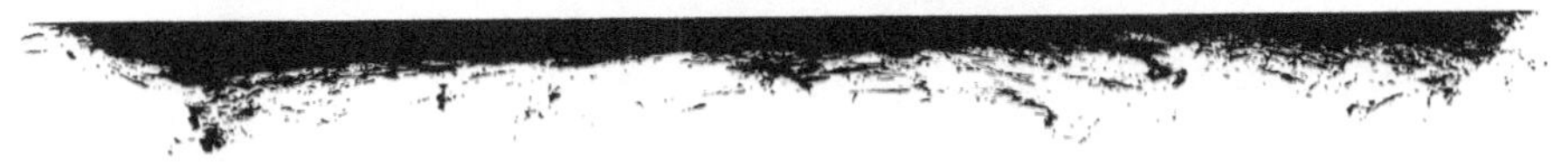

CONTENTS

I FELL ASLEEP ON THE SUBWAY AND MISSED MY STOP

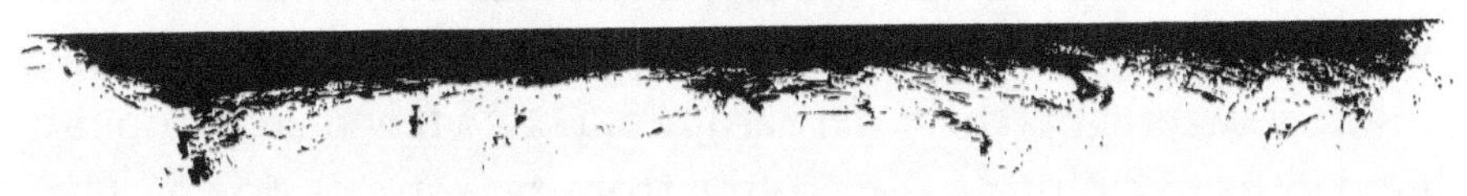

I'd lived in New York a few years, and was very familiar with the different subway lines, and felt no apprehension about staying out and drinking as much as I wanted on a Saturday evening. I had a long work week and decided to ruffle my feathers more than usual over the weekend. Too much drinking had me reeling and I left the bar around 1:30 a.m., homeward bound. I hopped on the G at about 1:50, and soon fell asleep on my trip home from Greenpoint to Clinton Hill, where I currently lived. When the automated "doors closing" announcement jolted me awake, I cocked my head and tried to read the station's signs at the dark platform before the train sped off, but it was unfamiliar and I'd assumed I'd missed mine. I scanned the empty subway car realizing I was the only one in it.

I scratched my head as I noticed the digital display of upcoming and past stops, and none of them were right. Hall's Point, Blue Lane, Carlson Ave, Reed Square, these were not stops on the G train, they were not stops in NYC on any line as far as I was aware. I felt a bit panicked, and the next subway we'd land at, I decided to leave the station to use my GPS and figure out where exactly I had mistakenly ended up. As we pulled into a station called "Rembault Ave", I exited the train and walked under the flickering yellow lights of the run down station towards the stairs, noticing then how barren it was. No other people exited the train or even appeared to be riding it.

I checked my phone; it was 2 a.m. and I had no service, so I climbed the stairs and felt the fall wind hit my face, a burning plastic smell mingling with the cold night's air. I looked around and was bewildered. I recognized nothing and it was a little unsettling how few streetlights there were around. I saw a few sketchy looking hooded teens pointing over to me from two streets down. They were sitting on a bench but got up and started walking slowly towards me. I felt uneasy and thought it likely these kids might try to rob me, so I headed down the steps again and swiped my card at the turnstile, getting an error. I tried again to no avail, and then hopped the rusty turnstile and descended the steps to the yellow tiled platform to wait for the next train.

I still had no chance to check my GPS, as the risk of losing my phone altogether if I was robbed was too great. I tried leaning near the stairs to get some signal but eventually gave up and waited for the train to arrive. After a few minutes I heard some coughing, and at the end of the platform I saw the three teenagers who'd been loitering outside, approach. They had their hoods covering their faces and were whispering while walking in my direction, heads fixed ahead. Panic turned to terror as I noticed the flash of a small, poorly concealed blade in one of the teen's gloved hands. I heard the rumble of the tracks and knew a train was approaching. I walked away, slowly at first, but gaining momentum as I heard their whispers getting closer. As the train car pulled up to the stop, I jumped on, praying they wouldn't follow on board. I watched while chills poured through me as they entered the adjacent car and worked their way down the aisle in my direction.

My panicked eyes darted to the upcoming stops: Craney Height's, 114th Street, Pebbler's Point. I was tired and had been drinking, but the approaching teens and the nonsensical subway stops drained everything from me except the dread and terror flooding my panicked mind. I saw the emergency brake and was about to run to it when the train screeched to a halt, arriving at a stop, painful metal squeals abrasively strained my ear drums. I stumbled forward and saw the ensuing teens sway before opening the door to the car I was in. Just then, the subway doors opened as the train stopped at whatever station it claimed to be. They charged me and I waited until nearly the last second before literally diving out of the closing doors. They closed on my shoe, which was now wedged between the metal sliding doors.

The teens were now pulling on the doors to open them and that's when I saw their faces. They looked emaciated and gaunt, eye sockets sharp around their inset, suffering eyes. They were filled with desperation and they looked sick and on the verge of death. The one with the blade drew it out and stabbed down on my shoe, puncturing it fractions of a second after I pulled my foot away. The door eventually closed, popping my shoe into the train, which sped off with the three ravenous attackers.

I caught my breath and walked under the flickering yellow lights and past grimy yellow tiled walls up to the stairs that left the station. "Craney's Heights", wherever this was, looked horrific. There were low-rise apartment buildings staggered throughout the heavily littered neighborhood. Fast food cartons for unrecognizable restaurant chains like "Bradley Burger" scattered the ground. My cellphone had no service, no bars, and even displayed a "Mobile network not available" message. I began to panic; I had no idea where I was, and then I saw glossy, black eyes peering at me from the apartment buildings. Emaciated faces just stared at me from the shadows of unlit rooms. I hurried back down the subway stairs and hopped the turnstile and waited for a train. Once aboard I rode and watched each unrecognizable station pass by: Wendell Yards, Brokov Center, and C Street, nothing even vaguely familiar.

Eventually I drifted off to sleep, and when I woke the train car had more people on it, all wasted away and distant. My phone had died and I had no way of determining the time. I asked some of the passengers about familiar stops such as Union Square or Barclay Center and nobody seemed to have any clue what I was saying. People seemed confused and unwilling to engage in conversation altogether. Eventually I followed a large group of people leaving to a bustling hub connecting the H lines, K lines and C2 through C8.

The city was not the one I'd known. Many things looked similar but everything and everyone I knew did not. I couldn't use my money, as it was called counterfeit by a bitter, whispering man in a shack-like newspaper stand that seemed to sell only small food items. My bank cards didn't work in the few, heavily damaged and old looking ATM machines I'd encountered. I eventually slept in the subway and then began to beg.

Everybody looks at me like I'm insane and homeless, and I am now, but I know I came from a different New York than this one I'm stuck in. I just pray I can get back somehow. I've been followed and stalked by other sickly looking people in hoodies and I only have coins an old man put in the coffee cup I found yesterday as I begged to cold eyes and nonspeaking wide stares. He only said one thing when placing the odd looking nickels in my cup, an unrecognizable large, bald man on the coins face. He whispered, "Don't let them know," before he vanished into a crowd of miserable looking commuters in grey and tattered clothing, leaving me in this foreign, starving city that is not my own.

It's been days, possibly weeks, of roaming the stations and the dark, low tenement buildings outside. I've never seen the sun, so time is a bit unclear. I've been living off of scraps, tiny gray pieces of shriveled meat I hope to god is chicken, and moldy buns from cardboard boxes branded with logos of nonexistent fast food spots. The filth and grime of the benches, spilled food and thick dust, has been accumulating on my filthy clothes as I sit, beg and sleep. I beg for anything from these miserable commuters, but rarely get a response, and I've been losing my voice as my body becomes weaker. I've caught my reflection in the window of a subway car and I look too thin; my body is eating its muscle. I saw someone today who looked out of place and very confused. I wanted to talk to him but he fled as I approached him, exiting the stairwell of Rembault station. Next time I see him, I'll make him stop. I found a car antenna and have been sharpening it. I'll do whatever it takes to get his phone and figure out how to get back home.

THE DELIVERY MAN WON'T LEAVE

It had just become dark when the door buzzer jolted me out of a lazy binge-watching session. I was alone in the apartment and had already received my delivery of Thai food, which sat half-eaten in a Styrofoam tray on my chair. I wasn't expecting anybody, and assumed it was a solicitor, but headed over to the intercom nonetheless. I asked, "Who is it?" slightly annoyed, but trying not to sound rude. There was a low muffled response; it sounded like someone was talking through a gag, or with an overly full mouth. I explained I couldn't understand and again asked who it was. The same, deep muffled voice answered with a mumbling. Not a single identifiable word erupted through the intercom, making me uneasy and waking me up with a strange chill. I walked over to the window overlooking the street and stared down.

Twenty odd feet below on the sidewalk in front of my door, was a rather tall, hunched man holding a very large cardboard box that looked like it fell out of a plane and into a landfill. There were dark, oily stains on it and crushed edges and haphazard strips of packing tape that looked like the only thing keeping it together. I had placed no recent orders, as I had been trying to curb my spending, but even if I had there was no way I was opening the door. The tall man's face was completely obscured by the large box, which he was holding high in front of his chest, clearly to hide his face intentionally. All I could see was the box and his hands that were covered in loosely hanging, blue palmed gardening gloves that appeared filthy and ill-fitting. Something about them seemed odd and misshapen. I stepped back slowly as my heart thudded in my chest. I walked back to the door and spoke firmly through the intercom, "Sorry, but that is not mine; I ordered nothing. Try the neighbors. Goodbye." I double-checked the deadbolt to ensure it was locked. I then walked back to my room, which felt uncomfortably exposed, and I shut my bedroom door as well. I un-paused my program and continued watching when the buzzer rang again in three long and jarring rings.

My heart raced again and I clenched my fingers until my knuckles whitened, walking again to the street side window. The tall man was still there, uneasily twitching the blue, denim cap that covered the top of his mostly-concealed head. Something about his head seemed misshapen, but I couldn't quite tell what because of the way he was hiding it with that large, stain-covered cardboard package. I backed up once more and walked over to the intercom, pressing the talk button. I told the man I was not accepting the package or opening the door, and if he didn't vacate immediately I'd be calling the police. My voice was shaky even though I'd tried to sound as intimidating as possible. I walked over to the window again and saw him standing there, unmoving, aside from an occasional tic or shiver.

I shivered as if in response, and then realized how cold I was. I adjusted the thermostat, which was on 78 when I heard a buzzer again, but muffled and distant, and certainly not my buzzer. It was my next door neighbor's and I was getting ready to text for advice when I heard a dreaded sound: the door lock release button buzzing as if mocking me. I slid my eye to the peephole and soon the tall man and his battered package crept into view in front of my door. I watched as my next door neighbor Dan's door opened behind him. I saw the look of both disgust and horror twist Dan's face as he scrambled inside and slammed the door. I heard the locks quickly latch behind him.

The man at the door turned slightly in response and I saw a sliver of the deformed face. It was massively elongated, as if there was a football sized tumor growing in the front of his skull, pressing it outward at a shocking angle. Slender, yellow teeth jutted outward like tiny tusks from the ovular frill-lipped mouth, which was a wide circle of agony that extended nearly half a foot in front of where it should. Under the stark shadows of the overhanging fluorescent lighting, I can safely say that nothing chilled my blood as much as that deformed and twisted face, and the watery grey eyes that sat in the elongated and stretched eye sockets.

The door handle jiggled roughly and loudly, and as the figure pounded hard on the door with the bottom of his gloved fist, I let out an involuntary gasp. Eyes wide with fear, I covered my mouth with both of my shaking hands and stepped backwards, nearly collapsing to the ground as terror wrought my body. The loud pounding continued for a few seconds before stopping, but as I nearly got my bearings, a thunderous crack jarred the door and I saw a tiny sliver of what could only be an axe blade piercing through.

I slid to the ground, mind spinning with the horror of the situation. My shaking hand removed the phone and I dialed 911 as quickly as it would allow, as another shocking blow to the door splintered a sizable chunk out of it. I scampered backwards, as if imitating a crab into the bedroom, where I kicked the door shut as an operator picked up. I told them in the stammering voice of a shock victim that a man was breaking in with an axe, trying to kill me, and I gave them my address. I heard the front door snap forward with a tremendous crash into the bedroom door in front of me. I was freezing, and wondering if I was having a heart attack, nearly praying for that rather than the other impending death that opened my bedroom door and looked at me with those unnatural grey blobs of eyes.

His face was beyond anything I'd seen in documentaries about facial tumors, beyond anything I'd seen in horror movies, just a shocking vulgar deformation of anything remotely human. The long stretched slits of nostrils trailed down to those tusks, and below that the maw that looked incapable of eating revealed a massive red lump that might have been a tongue just behind the jutting teeth. I was frozen in place as the tall figure charged over to me and I squeezed my eyes shut, preferring darkness to the horror in front of me to be my last memory if I was going to die. I felt a whoosh of air as the man hurriedly stepped over me. I heard a sickening wet whack, like a pumpkin splitting, and my fingers climbed up to the top of my head, ready to find it split in two.

A groan drifted into silence somewhere behind me and I felt long, bony and misshapen gloved fingers pull my arm gently. I opened my eyes to the deformed man attempting to pull me to my feet, and saw the gloved hand pointing behind me. I looked over to the open window I'd sworn I'd closed earlier, to where the gloved hand pointed to the crumpled figure beside my bed, to the other large man dressed in black lying in a pool of blood from an axe wound in his chest, to that long, serrated knife in his black, gloved fingers by his side. It was the home invader, a deranged murderer that this deformed man had seen breaking into my apartment. This deformed man turned out to be my shut in neighbor, Jeremy, from the apartment building behind mine, Jeremy to whom I owed my life.

THE CLICKING SOUND COMING FROM OUR NEW CAT...

My parents owned the same cat my entire life, Bubs, an adorable orange tabby who lived outdoors more often than in. I grew up in a quaint little town in Maine that was stunningly beautiful, with crashing waves, endless moody skies and plenty of grassy places to bound about and climb trees, as both children and their outdoor cats do. Bubs was always there for me, purring on my lap and rubbing against my ankles when returning from a frolic in the woods. As I grew into a teenager, he stayed the same size and aged gracefully, but one day he went missing. I asked my father, who broke the news; he'd been hit by a car and been killed. My mother was deeply distraught, more so than I, and I tried to cheer her up. The next week she had a sad, distant look about her, until nearly a month after when she found the kitten.

We'd been on a walk along the rocks of a nearby bay shore on a particularly windy day, just about a half hour from our house, when we heard the cry. An adorable gray kitten emerged from some tall grass, mewing and sniffing at our feet with a high pitched, heart-melting little voice. He looked to be about three months old and had a dappling of black spots on his back. My mom picked him up and gazed at him with her loving eyes as only she could so perfectly do, for the four-legged stranger. Dad raised an eyebrow at me and smiled. No words needed to express what we both knew: we had a new pet cat.

Pip, as my mom had been referring to him over the next few days, was an adorable new friend, but he sometimes made a strange clicking sound. It was almost always when he was conked out or asleep, and wasn't loud exactly, but it was pretty odd. I asked my mom about it and she just chalked it up to the ocean air, but something about it seemed off and actually creeped me out a bit. He'd be walking around, playing with string, and then would plop down for a nap and that sound would bubble up out of him instead of a snore, which I would have been more than happy to listen to. The clicking just seemed so out of place. Mom was back to her joyous self, though, so I tried not to dwell on it. The next few days I'd wished I only had an off-putting clicking to deal with.

Around the fifth day, the proud cat owners we'd returned to being, I'd noticed some peculiar behavior. Pip would occasionally move in a rapid kind of scuttling that seemed so unnatural and foreign for a cat. I'd looked up cat videos to try and see what kind of condition this might be. I discovered something called Feline Cerebellar Hypoplasia, an issue with an underdeveloped cerebellum, but even that looked far different from the rapid movements he'd make. On top of that, he was clicking more often, and the putrid stink of his litter box seemed to hang on him at all times. I'd told my mom once she finally returned from the post office (where she works), and she just told me with a smile to, "Give him a bath, silly."

I walked over and picked him up, and realized he felt unhealthy, very bony. I frowned but took him to the tub and began to wash him. I coated him twice with shampoo but he still had a lingering stink. I finally gave up and when I went to pick him out of the water I screamed in pain and stared at my bleeding finger. There was a straight slice in it, not a bite like I was expecting. I shook him angrily (not too hard, and yes I felt horrible about doing so), and he stared at me with his unfeeling black orbs of eyes and began to make that awful clicking sound again. I kept my distance when drying him with a towel, again confused at how he felt so bony, but was the same size the entire time we'd had him. I began staying clear of Pip.

On Monday, after about three days of avoidance aside from the odor, which even caused my mom to purchase some Yankee candles for the house, my father expressed concern. Mom realized this was abnormal so we'd made a vet appointment on her first day off, that Thursday. I saw Pip peering at me under the table during dinner that night, and as I cleared the table to wash dishes, he made some violent crunching motion, like he was compacting from front to back. It made my heart skip a beat, causing the blood to drain from my face. It was completely unnatural, like a compressing accordion, and I ran in horror to my parent's room where they assured me the vet would take care of whatever was wrong. I tried to explain this wasn't me overreacting, but there seemed to be no way to convince her. Upon exiting her room, I saw Pip sitting calmly and staring at me with those bulging black eyes. They seemed to be pulsating slightly, or almost jutting outward, and the entire room smelled of the acrid stench of death. I ran to my room, not taking my eyes off of him. I locked my door that night for the first time.

Today, I awoke to the muffled sound of crying and entered the living room to find my mother in tears. On the carpet beside her lay the lifeless body of Pip, but it looked like he'd been slaughtered violently, deflated and split. There was a trail of blood leading from his back end that faded out after a few feet, and there were tiny footprints in the drying blood on the carpet. They were claw prints; I swear they looked like lobster claw prints, or more so a crab. I tried to console my mom and said, "He was sick and it wasn't our fault", but she shook her head, face strained with despair, and said she didn't care about the cat. She just motioned a limp arm towards the kitchen after wiping away tears from her eyes. I slowly walked over, following the direction of trailing blood to meet my father's blank eyes staring at me, and listened in utter horror as he slowly opened his mouth wide and made the familiar sound of clicking.

BRITTLEWOOD ESTATES

I have no idea who to turn to and where to go, but I need to get this out there in case someone else has experienced it too. I had a decent apartment with a great roommate in New York, a good job and great coworkers who I hung with after work on occasion. I had a wonderful girlfriend of three years and a great relationship with my family. As of Monday morning, everything has been changing and I have no idea why. I woke up, and after my morning coffee and a quick bagel, I headed to the subway. I received a random email, looking like spam labeled: "Congratulations! You've been selected..." I didn't read it, just clicked the "opt out and unsubscribe" button and kept walking, surprised at a lack of other emails I usually received about whatever meetings or projects were ongoing.

I boarded the subway car and received a very unwelcoming stare, almost of disgust by a passenger across from me. After a few minutes of him leering at me, I stood up and moved. I then stood near a young girl who was perhaps in her 20s, who did a double take and soon walked away from me to the other side of the car. Confused, thinking that I had maybe cut myself shaving and was bleeding, I took out my phone and switched the camera to face me.

Nothing, just my normal self. I shook my head in disbelief and went to work as usual.

My coworkers were quiet that day; there was no small talk or any interaction until I mentioned grabbing lunch and got no response. I was confused so I asked again and got an eye roll from my normally chatty co-worker, Beth. This was really eating away at me, so I went to the bathroom to check a mirror. Once there I looked up and down closely. Nothing was on my face, my back, or, hoping I hadn't soiled myself unknowingly, my rear. Relieved at a lack of fluids of any sort on my body, I returned to my desk and continued working until the end of the day, when I received an email from my boss informing me that I was terminated and needn't come in the next day. I was enraged and shocked, but I calmly walked over to his office to ask what was going on.

He could barely make eye contact with me and said, "I'm not spelling it out for you," before threatening to call security if I didn't leave. Was a lookalike running my name through the mud? Did I black out and drunk call my boss insulting him? I looked at my outgoing calls, emails, texts, and there was nothing at all. I rushed to the subway in tears and headed back home, everybody still glaring, home to my girlfriend, Ann.

Upon arriving, I opened the door to find Ann packing her stuff with an angry, disgusted look. "What is going on!?" I pleaded, but I received no answer. I tried to get her to stop and talk but she pushed my arms down and stormed out without a single word. I felt cursed; nothing made sense and the aggression from everyone was overwhelming. I called my mother but after one ring it was cut short, ignored. I tried multiple times and got the same reaction. Freaking out, I texted my friends, but there was no response. I called them and all of the calls were ignored.

I slept horribly after crying myself to sleep and awoke to go get breakfast. My coffee store ignored my order and refused to sell me anything, and grocery stores and bodegas were doing the same: shirt, shoes, but no service. They just waved knives or bats and told me to leave before they called the cops. My stomach was knotted with hunger and I began to fear for my well-being. After roaming the streets that day, my hunger drove me to pick up a half-eaten sandwich out of the trash. I felt like the lowest rung in all of civilization and thought things couldn't get any worse. That night, however, they did.

I returned to my apartment to find the locks changed. I looked up to see if my roommate, Dave, was home. He was, but was glowering at me with the most hateful eyes I'd seen before shutting the blinds. Then I felt it, a sharp pain in my right arm. I looked at it to see it was cut, blood was blossoming across the sleeve of my shirt. A middle aged woman was standing next to me with a bloody knife, squinted eyes and a sneering face. I grabbed my bleeding arm and ran, then noticing the others. *Every* single person I could see on the street was approaching, many holding improvised weapons ranging from bats to rocks. My heart was fluttering and I ran as far and as fast as I could towards the docks a few miles away. Eventually I outran the mob of crazed attackers after one pegged me in the face with a large rock when I'd sprinted by.

I waited for hours and resorted to eating some raw, rotting fish I found on the pier that was likely used for bait. Starving and cold, I nestled under a bench to hide and block the wind. I tried to make sense of it all, then realized the only communication I'd had that wasn't terrible was that spam email I'd received. I opened it up and read over it. It was sent from not an email address, but rather a string of what seemed to be random characters. It read: "Congratulations! You have automatically been added to a list of winners. Best regards, Dan Reverton, CCO Brittlewood Estates". There was no website, no address or phone number, no explanation of what this company did, why they existed, and how or whether they made money. On the bottom in small print read, "Click here to change subscription options". I clicked it, fingers numbing in the fall night. I received a "renewal confirmed!" email with no explanation otherwise.

I eventually passed out and woke to a police officer asking me if I was all right. He offered me a ride and I agreed. I was relieved to have a person interacting with me normally as I'd been so alienated and aggressively attacked over the past few days. I reached the apartment, and my roommate was there explaining he'd changed the locks due to a creepy loitering man. He had no recollection of anything relating to me, however, nor did anyone else I texted, called or spoke to. My boss even asked why I was late, forgiving me when I lied saying I'd needed to change the locks for my roommate.

Everything seemed normal for the next 24 hours and all seemed fine; there were no hateful looks or attacks. It wasn't until the next evening when I received an email with the title "Pass on the Winnings!"

Upon opening it, the email read: "Pass on the winnings to keep your subscription! Just forward this to a friend!" I contemplated long and hard and thought of someone who did me wrong who I still had the email contact for. I had no desire to hurt them, so I added a message explaining to them it was urgent not to unsubscribe or opt out, but upon clicking "send" the email had changed entirely, lacking my addition. It now seemed to read: "Congratulations! You have automatically been added to a list of winners. Best regards, Dan Reverton, CCO Brittlewood Estates," and the email address associated with it wasn't mine, but simply a string of random characters. I don't remember sending this email, but it's to someone that I think I hate. Someone I really hate. Someone I really, really want to hurt...

WHY ARE THEY BRINGING ME THEIR LEGS?

So, here is the backstory. I am a pretty normal child from a lower middle class family. I grew up near the woods and there was very little to do, as my mother hired a babysitter to watch us (actually the TV). My sister and I were creative in figuring out how to entertain ourselves. We'd build forts, draw, play tag and whatnot. Our house was a bit old and the attic, where we often played, had a lot of daddy longlegs spiders. We weren't sadists in any other regard, but I was unfortunately guilty of ripping off their legs (I was about five, my sister seven at the time). This was a short phase we quickly abandoned as we grew up, went to school, then college, and then graduated to the job world.

The rest of my life I've owned a cat and then a dog, and have never hurt anything except swatting mosquitoes (which I think is fair game). I recently moved into an older building and noticed a daddy longlegs spider walking about. I had a flashback of sorts and used a cup to capture and free it outside the apartment. I thought nothing of it, until I woke the next day and used the bathroom. I was about to brush my teeth when I looked in the mirror and saw a thin black line on my lip. I was taken aback, thinking I had a cut when I realized it was a thin insect leg. I wiped it away and washed my face thoroughly before heading off to work. I was a bit repulsed but didn't make much of it, as I assumed there was a dead one that I'd rolled onto during the night.

A few days passed before I saw another one. I was home unwinding with a beer and the television when I saw it out of the corner of my eye. There was a daddy longlegs spider slowly approaching me. Something seemed off about it though, and as I bent down to observe I saw it was carrying one of its detached hind legs in its mouth. I watched as it slowly approached, and then freaked out a little bit, scooping it with a piece of paper and rushing to the apartment entrance to toss it outside. I was a bit grossed out and immediately called the landlord to complain. The exterminator would come the following day, he said, and so I did an extensive search to make sure no bugs were in my room before finally relaxing and falling asleep that night.

The next day I woke to an irritating cough, wiped something off my mouth, and bolted to the bathroom. There were *dozens* of spider legs in my mouth between my gums and my teeth. I completely lost it. I brushed, rinsed, flossed, mouth-washed, and repeated the process over and over, holding back tears and trying to avoid a full on panic attack. I was half an hour late after cleaning my mouth and calling my landlord expressing the urgency until finally reaching him. After he swore to me the exterminator was arriving that day, I took a train to work but achieved very little. I was googling everything to understand what was going on, researched their behavior, looked on message boards, but found nothing even remotely similar to what was happening to me. I became more confused and was nauseated to the point of skipping lunch. I called the landlord to verify the exterminator had sprayed before even considering returning to the apartment. I looked everywhere: behind the couch, in cupboards, and even in the bathtub drain to make sure there were no signs of them.

The next day I awoke and was relieved to have nothing anywhere near my face resembling spider legs. I sighed, releasing the ball of stress in my belly, and began making breakfast when I saw them on the floor. Three severed, gnarled rodent legs were resting in a crimson pool of blood on the floor near the trash cabinet. I flipped out and called the landlord, sending him a photo using my phone camera. He apologized and promised to come by that day to address it. I called out of work that day, too angry and disturbed to even try to work. I hit up a friend who lived nearby and asked to crash on the couch, explaining I had an infestation and that they needed to fumigate. After assuring him they were not bedbugs, he agreed, and I headed over to his place later that day. He seemed concerned, looking at me like I was insane as I told the story, but I showed him the photo of the rodent limbs and he was soon as dumbfounded as me. We shared some beers and the mood lightened. Eventually I crashed and slept like a baby for the first time in at least a week.

I woke up with a stretch and my heart sunk as I felt something on my mouth. I ran to the bathroom and in the mirror was shocked to see white hairs caked to my lips with blood. I washed it all off and went to knock on my friend's door when I heard some muffled sobbing. I knocked again and called for him, and when I heard no answer I pushed open the door to see him, hunched over the lifeless body of his cat. Both of its front legs were missing in a mangled mess that implied ripping or biting wounds. I tried to console him and he shouted at me, bulging eyes and raised fists. On the way out I saw drops of blood on the floor of the couch I'd slept on. I noticed a trail of blood as well. I called my parents, who calmed me down a bit, and who suggested "seeing someone". I agreed, when all of a sudden my stomach began stinging me with a sharp, acute pain. I bought antacids and Pepto, Advil and aspirin, but the pain wouldn't subside. Eventually I hailed a cab to take me to the ER. A few hours later a visibly concerned nurse informed me there were two entire cat legs blocking my digestive tract and that

I needed surgery. My stress levels were through the roof; I felt I looked like a monster but I knew I didn't perpetrate this. I imagined the possibility of sleepwalking but realized this was not the case a day later while recovering from my surgery.

The following day after being knocked out and operated on, I awoke gagging and dry heaving as something large was being shoved down my throat. It was a foot, a human foot. The patient sharing my room, a 72-year-old thyroid cancer patient, was shoving his freshly severed, thin and wrinkly leg into my mouth, yellow toenails, flecks of blood and all. I freaked out, shoved him, and called the nurse, who screamed and vomited immediately upon arrival. I was crying and punching at the man but he kept hopping forward and trying to feed me his severed leg before passing out from blood loss. I ripped out my IV drips and staggered out the door, crazed and terrified. Doctors shoved me aside to rush to the man's aid, the man who was now likely dead from his self-mutilation. I was cracking, my world a terrifying, unending nightmare, and tears were running down my face. The taste of the man's fungal feet were in my mouth, forcing me to gag as I ran towards the highway. I approached the nearby river and gazed into the black water, nearly considering suicide before finally calming down.

This was days ago, but I am not sure exactly how many, as I haven't slept. Delirium is setting in and I fear for what may happen if I slip into unconsciousness. I can think of no explanation and am on the verge of breaking down and doing something drastic. But then I saw it, like a neon beacon in the darkness. Crown Fried Chicken. I'm breaking in and sleeping there tonight. It's worth a shot...

THE FIELD IN THE PHOTOGRAPH

I was helping my mother clean out her house when I saw the photo on the wall. She'd decided to move to Florida to get some much needed sunshine and prepare for an early retirement, and I had nothing but the best wishes and utmost support for her. We'd grown up in a beautiful, rural town in Delaware with 12 acres of woods and a large field my sister and neighbors would play war and other games in. It was quiet and serene, and I had nothing to complain about; but when I saw the photo on the wall, an unease swept over me, and I felt a chill deep in my bones.

In the photo, my sister and I, ages six and nine, were covered in muddy clothing, smiling in the backyard. Behind the yard, the sprawling yellow field was visible, with white skies overhead without even the faintest blush of blue. It was just a colorless gray sky that always hung over the field regardless of the sun. Tall, dead-looking reeds grew wild in the wavy field that ended at the tree line to thick woods. The photo was taken in the fall, as it was the day I saw the photo, and as it had been in the distant and dark memory that flooded back with the scent of distant leave piles burning in the crisp air.

My sister and I joked about running away occasionally, and one day we tried building a fort in that field nearly 30 years ago.

We'd been barely staying upright in the intense wind that fall had delivered, and as hunger set in, we decided to call it quits and abandon our pyramid of branches until the following day. As we walked back towards the house, I noticed a tall bulge in the earth in the distance, roughly, five feet tall and eight feet in diameter. It was a bit unnatural and something about it stirred a sense of uneasiness as if it had no reason to be there. For many years, an occasional reminder of the field woke a lingering fear in me, but I didn't remember why. All I knew was that something about that mound in the field made me shake in my skin.

The following day we did not return to the field to finish our fort and new home away from home. We'd learned our neighbor, Andy, an eight-year-old kid, was missing, and the police somberly informed us that they suspected foul play. He'd been playing outside and had just vanished. As days turned to weeks, it became clear that he'd likely been abducted and the chances of him being found alive were increasingly slim. Adding to the unease in the neighborhood, a few months later a different neighbor's horse got loose from its fenced area and was never found or even spotted anywhere.

My father got a better job in Pittsburgh as summer arrived, and we left the old house. We then left Pittsburgh for college and life began to unfold into jobs, better jobs, careers, and soon I was a full time operations manager of a major law firm. All was normal and fine until I saw that photo again and what I can only describe as a repressed memory tumbled loose and I remembered. I remembered the reason for turning back in that field and staring at the unnatural lump in the ground. I remembered a low, bass gurgling sound that sent me running at top speed back towards my sister and the house.

I'm not a superstitious man by any means and I feel it's important to emphasize this. I do not believe in ghosts, vampires, monsters, aliens or 9/11 conspiracy theories, or even Murphy's Law. This is the reason I decided to go back: to try to make sense of what had caused this unfathomable dread about the considerably beautiful field of my childhood home. I asked my mother about the field the day I helped her move, and her only comment was that there had been some septic runoff back there, which accounted for the greener grass and excessive weeds in the back of the field. This might explain the gurgling sound as well, of course, but as much as I tried to convince myself it was a childhood imagination run rampant, the less I believed it. I called my sister the next day and she had absolutely no memory of anything out of the ordinary in the field except a stench of sewage.

I decided to carry on with my affairs, working ten-hour days in Chicago and meeting with some very high-profile future clients. The following week I'd secured a meeting with a son of a very famous architect and was to fly to Delaware. I decided I'd take a later return flight in order to pay a visit to the old house since I was in the area. My mother had left some things in the old storage shed she'd asked me to sort through, and I insisted on helping. I wanted to see the field again and try to wrap my head around the brooding fear I never came to terms with.

The meeting went wonderfully. I was 90% positive we'd sealed the account, and I had a bounce in my step that day. I drove the company car down the windy, narrow roads into the country and eventually to Shiloh Church Road, down the drive to my old child-hood home, laughing in my head that I was just a little scaredy-cat back then. I smiled to myself, but there was a thick unease through-out my mind. I noticed a "For Sale" sign prominent in the front lawn. My parents had sold the house, and it appeared that the next owners had as well. It was nothing too surprising, but again, another premonition kept pointing to the idea that something did not sit right.

I could tell the place was uninhabited, as there were no cars, blinds or any furniture on the property. I gripped my cell phone tightly and stared beyond the house into the tall grass of the field, dead except for the back near the woods where there was a dash of bright green that almost appeared painted on. My steps led me closer and closer and I saw the mound. I tried to fight off a shiver as I approached but was unable.

It was larger. I know this because everything I returned to since childhood was tiny, and even our old house looked like a scaled down model from the massive abode I'd previously known. The mound seemed to be 18 feet in diameter and maybe 10 feet in height. It almost looked like a natural feature of the land from a distance, but as I moved closer it looked freakishly out of place and simply wrong in every way. I trudged towards it, unaware of my footing until I was a few yards from it.

My shoes had sunk into some septic murk, suctioning up mud as I walked ever closer. Every hair on my body stood on end as I heard a bass, guttural croak popping from the mound. I stepped back but my shoe stuck in place and slipped off of my foot. I noticed some sort of twitching from the side and my mind tried to comprehend what was moving. It looked like an animal of some sort, with no legs or head, about the size of a small dog. The end came to a black cylindrical shape, and after a few minutes of trying to understand what I was seeing I realized it was the grotesquely engorged leg of a horse, nearly a foot in diameter and maybe five feet in length.

It was grey and slimy, barely visible in the luscious grasses and weeds covering the mound. Dark black veins spasmed under the putrid flesh, and my gaze followed them upward into the mound's mass, which I then realized was covered in black, slowly pulsating veins as well. I became quite lightheaded, smelling something both septic and chemical, and I slapped myself hard to prevent myself from blacking out. My eyes followed the veins in their strange latticed pattern, observing unidentifiable blobs and pulsating nodules that slowly leaked thick, blackish brown chunks of some material I had no desire to understand. I slowly stepped backwards as I noticed the heads.

At first they looked like featherless bird heads poking out the front of the mound, but then I realized they were noses, a large cluster of them, writhing barely visibly under the thick grass on the mound. They seemed neither dead nor alive, gray translucent flesh that writhed unnaturally as if inhabited by another host. The hollow eye sockets above them were filled with grass, nearly hiding them completely. They were human heads, or at least portions of them, overlaid on top of each other like sloppily stacked quivering masks. I realized then that both my shoes were missing and my next steps backward stripped my socks away with the cold, sludgy mud beneath the grass.

I couldn't turn away from the horror, but I needed to get away with a desperation that only the knowledge of impending death can summon. I felt a stinging sensation on my muddy bare feet that grew with every slow and difficult step. The sting turned to burn and the next excruciating step had me screeching so loudly that my voice croaked to a wheeze. I clawed at the painfully acidic muddy grass further away and used every muscle in my body to rip myself from the oozing captivity of the hazy field, a lingering mist vaguely screening the maddening scene. I saw the glaze of mucous-like blood mixing with the mud on my hands and forced myself to keep from fainting yet again. I kept staring back at the mound and I swore it was following me as I moved.

The faces seemed more prominent now, contorting and making unnatural expressions, as whatever thing that kept them somewhat intact manipulated them. I thought about calling the authorities but knew I'd be overtaken by the time I could dial. I kept clawing my way backwards, skin burning, and felt the pop of a finger separate at the final joint on my dissolving, foamy pinkie finger, then on my other hand. I forced myself to look away from the thing in the field, and after 10 endless minutes of painful struggling that felt like an eternity, I was on the backyard grass of my childhood home, my arms and legs red, stripped down almost to the muscle on my bloody hands and feet. I rolled as far as I could the rest of the way until reaching the driveway and dialed 911 before succumbing to the pain. I heard police sirens then fell unconscious.

I remember nothing except waking up in my childhood hospital, where I'd spent some time after a broken leg as a kid. The room was empty but I saw a policeman sitting outside the door. A nurse eventually entered and informed me I'd lost a pinkie and half of another, as well as three of my toes but that otherwise I should make a speedy recovery, scarred but functional. I asked about the field and received no information as the nurse walked away in a rush.

A few hours later the policeman out front asked me questions about chemicals, drug labs, lye, methamphetamine production and hallucinogens. I explained in the only way I could to not sound insane, that there was some sort of corrosive chemical in the field that I'd stepped into while trying to examine the damage from a septic leakage. I explained I had dialed 911 just before passing out. The cop sneered at me and told me three officers were missing, assumed dead, and that one was his partner. He swore he'd crucify me the moment he got confirmation of what he was sure I'd done to them. Apologies and explanations were pointless, as he wasn't hearing it.

A few days later the hospital released me, and having no evidence of any wrongdoing on my part, I was free and so I returned to my career in Chicago. I tried to explain what happened to my sister and she told me she was concerned about my mental health. She offered to check out the field with me to help put whatever troubled event I'd been suppressing since childhood to rest, insinuating molestation or domestic violence. I told her to stay away from there if she wanted to prevent any more suffering and I felt assured that she had no interest in going anywhere near the field after I made her swear to stay away. I doubt anybody will ever take me seriously. I almost prefer that, that is, unless you live on Shiloh Church Road. And if you do, I can only beg you to stay away from that field.

STRIDULATION

I've been in New York a few years, and at night, and on a few occasions had to deal with the unfortunate gap between trains after 2 a.m. that crawls time to a halt. Every odor magnifies and sounds that are usually masked by conversation, coughing, and train brakes are heard. Mostly, extreme boredom and a dying phone battery are the focus of these gaps, but occasionally I've heard sounds coming from the darkness in the train tunnels. I assumed these sounds to be a worker or machinery, but last night something sounded both different and familiar that I couldn't quite wrap my head around.

Last night I was freezing, having forgotten my jacket, as I'd assumed the unexpectedly warm fall weather would continue. It was windy and I was unfortunately wearing just a thin t-shirt as I waited for what felt like hours for my train back home. My teeth continued chattering and I tucked my hands under my armpits to try to warm up. I heard something that sounded like my own teeth rattling from the intense chill, deep from the recesses of the train tunnel. I tilted my head in curiosity, angling my ears towards the eerie sound. A feeling of a wave of unease tingled my skin, and so I walked away from the direction of the sound to stand on the other end of the platform. The air from the chilly night was blowing through the ventilation grates, and I realized that until the train arrived, the cold was inescapable. I checked my dead phone, trying to find comfort in staring at a screen, lit and functional or not. It was probably around 3 a.m. by then, and I wanted nothing more than to crawl into my bed, away from the wind that blew through me and frosted my bones, away from that chattering that seemed to be mimicking my own in response.

Eventually I sat on a wooden bench, tucking my hands under my cool jeans. After a few more minutes I'd noticed a kid at the other end of the platform. I hadn't noticed him before, and I was honestly relieved as I realized his own teeth to be the source of the sound. He looked to be about eight or nine, and underdressed as well. I smiled and said, "We didn't dress warm enough for tonight, huh," trying to break the awkward silence between the only two souls at the station. He looked over at me and cocked his head as if unable to understand. I then froze as I heard his chattering intensify, becoming louder than I imagined possible for a young boy's teeth to possibly make.

It was a quick burst, and then it stopped as if controlled, unlike my own rapid clacking teeth. He seemed unaware of the cold, his arms loosely hanging at his side as he swayed in place a bit strangely. He approached shyly, walking slowly towards me in between hiding behind the platform pillars. I thought it was cute and tried to smile, although I felt a bit uncomfortable. "Where are your parents? It's pretty late to be out alone," I said before breathing hot air into my cupped hands. He peeked out again from a pillar, looking confused. It is New York, so there was always the chance he knew no English.

My teeth chattered again as I was unable to control my jaw, and in response the boy let out a loud vibratory sound, though now I saw that his mouth was open in curious confusion, teeth unable to have been the cause of that rattling like mine. I then noticed his shoulders; they twitched backwards as he made the sound in a rapid quiver that looked unnatural, almost insect-like. I then watched with a mixture of horror and awe as the boy turned to peer into the tunnel, and I watched as his shoulder blades connected together in a rapid clattering. They were elongated and exposed skeleton, poking through clearly worn holes in the back of his ancient Spiderman t-shirt.

The boy turned back to me, head cocked as if awaiting a response, and as my teeth clicked with my uncontrollable shivering I saw a look of curiosity turn to horror as his mouth and eyes widened in a horrific contortion after noticing my teeth being the source of the sound. He stepped back and let out a loud stream of noise, stridulation from his scapula that echoed off the tile walls in the large chamber of the station. I backed slowly and heard the ominous, deep buzzing sound swell from the black subway tunnel as dozens of droning adult males exited the tunnel in a deafening clatter, lumbering into the light and quickening in swaying steps, climbing the platform then rushing towards me with an awkward and increasing speed. I stared in terror at the wide, white eyes and veiny, pale skin, much like tissue paper, on the mass of adults arising from the black depths of the tunnel. I sprinted up the stairs as quickly as possible and into the chilling wind of the street.

I was eventually able to hail a cab, eventually able to return home, and after hours of lying in bed trying to slow my pulse, was eventually able to go to sleep. Today even felt like a normal day: coffee and toast, my routine resumed. I likely might have been able to enjoy the weekend, that is, until I stopped at the store. On my way to the bodega a few blocks down, I heard the sound that chilled my bones to the marrow. I looked down to see a pair of washed out white eyes staring intensely from the sewer grate. That thing that was almost but not quite human, was watching me.

STRENGTH POTIONS

Dave and I are immature for our age; I'm well aware of this fact. We get wild at shows and gross each other out, but for the most part it's all in good fun and nobody ever gets hurt. When our favorite band announced a show in upstate New York, we thought it was a good time to catch up and go camping on the way up the night before. We packed some steaks and beers, charcoal, tents and a tiny grill, and filled up the truck with gas at the station before heading out.

The drive up was great, sharing stories of loves lost, shows attended and projects of ours that never quite made it past the starting line. We had tried to start some bands but never really got them off the ground and ended up settling in our careers, he as a sound engineer and I a promoter. We'd been friends since the 5th grade, and he was by far my oldest and best. Dave remembered first as he just inserted a CD of his new favorite metal band, a bit too intense for my liking.

"Ha, ha, my god, remember Strength Potions?" he asked, and a flood of memories washed back as if they happened yesterday. As kids, we'd wager candy, comics, even dibs on girls (as if that was an option), on our ability to drink each other's vile, concocted beverage of our own invention. We'd propose beverages, promising to smell them to ensure nothing too vile passed the test, and that we'd drink a sip, cringing, screaming, vomiting or gagging before laughing riotously.

"Oh, yes, pretty unforgettable once you drink mayo and mud water," I replied, sounding as if I was trying my best not to vomit. We both laughed and tried to remember the worst concoctions, naming them back and forth in a reciprocating manner.

We'd invented the game (or so we thought) and named it after the saying: "Whatever doesn't kill you makes you stronger," but I'm pretty sure I almost died from dehydration a few times after puking my brains out over some of the worst *potions* we'd been unfortunate enough to create.

"Ketchup and milk," he offered.

"Tuna fish juice and milk," I stepped it up.

"Meatloaf TV dinner. Blended," he boasted.

"Oh, god, the rotten boiled Brussels sprout water," I coughed. "Ugh, I can still taste it."

"Didn't you drink urine and tomato juice?" he asked.

"No; I cheated on that one. Ha ha. I pretended to, but no way was I doing that."

"Don't blame you," he replied, and we cracked up like hyenas, howling in anticipation of our trip and happy to be in each other's immature company after over a year.

We arrived at the ground we intended to camp at; it was beautiful. Fall leaves scattered the tall trees with fiery hues and there was even a pretty blue moss on the wooded ground, making it soft and cushioned. We'd unpacked and set up our tents before clearing a place to set up a contained fire pit. As night was upon us, the yellow glow from the fire set the stage for stories of good and bad times. Beers were drank, he lit a joint, and he leaned over as if about to unveil an amazing secret, and I leaned in as he let one rip. I laughed, middle fingers up, and called him "the talented idiot pig". Eventually we called it a night and crawled into our respective tents and sleeping bags. My mouth was already hurting from smiling and laughing so hard and I was out of steam.

I woke up in the dead of night, the smoldering fire and plentiful stars dappling the night's sky. The vented screen in the front of the tent was covered, and the whole tent seemed smaller, compressed by... something. I pressed the roof up and felt the texture and weight from the other side. Confused, I zipped down the tent entrance, only to see a mesh of blue moss hanging over it completely, obscuring the view. I brushed it aside to call for Dave to check it out when I felt it move slightly. I quickly withdrew my hand, questioning my senses. In front of my eyes it curled slightly inward. "Dave, check this out," I called, but heard no response.

Fear began to set in and only heightened when I heard the heavy sucking sound, rhythmic like, and struggled breathing from outside the tent. I extended my hands to the top and shook the tent, knocking some of the moss from the canopy and revealing the view of Dave's tent, which was covered in the same sprawling blue moss and left slightly unzipped overnight. Dread filled me. I brushed the remaining moss aside from the tent and passed the carpet of blue to his tent.

I opened the zipper to see him slowly rocking back and forth in his sleeping bag with that felt-like blue moss completely covering his face like a velvet mask. I brushed at the moss, but as it lifted with resistance there was blood oozing out from underneath, popping out a deep chunk to reveal muscle. I let out a quick horrific shout; it had eaten and seemingly replaced the entirety of flesh on his face. I yelled his name, shook him, and he seemed out of it, emitting a grunting sound, breathing in labored, gurgling breaths. I reached for my phone, called 911, but we had no signal out there in the woods. Of course.

It was reaching up with tiny nubby tendrils in the firelight, this horrific moss. A sharp prick in my palm drew my attention to the thin blue spongy strands reaching into my skin. I brushed it off, fear intensely gathering adrenaline in my bloodstream. I stood to run but my guts churned and I fell immediately to my side grabbing my burning torso. I remembered the games before going to sleep, the drunken strength potions we'd concocted. I made him drink river water mixed with ketchup and pine needles. He'd had me drink beer mixed with mustard and some of that curious blue moss.

TENANT

I saw the ad on Craigslist: an apartment perfect for me location-wise as well as size. I was impressed and made an appointment for that afternoon. After work I knocked on the door in anticipation, and the landlord opened the door a crack, releasing a musty scent that caught me off guard. When he opened the door I was surprised at how small he was. Opened, I saw the amazing interior: full kitchen, an actual living room and even a back patio. I was ecstatic and said with a resounding smile before writing a check, "I'll take it!"

Mark, the landlord, was a thin man of few smiles, but he was pleasant enough, offering me a water which I needed, and let me get the keys to move in early. I shook his hand and smiled wide. It was finally a great place that wasn't an overpriced rip off. It was like everything was coming up Millhouse, and "Walking on Sunshine" played faintly in my head.

The next few days I'd brought a load of boxes over, as well as my mattress and box spring, couch and dresser, and moved in early, excited to have room to finally breathe in. I decorated the walls and countertops, loaded the fridge with groceries, the bathroom with cleaning supplies and toiletries. I slid on the wood flooring in my socks like a giddy child and cooked my first meal. It was wonderful. But then I heard a sound, a muffled, haunting sound from the wall.

It sounded almost like a generic moan of someone doing a poor ghost impersonation, and my mind suddenly flashed to a person wearing a sheet trying to be minimally scary. It wasn't too loud but I didn't like how I could hear through the walls. I merely turned on the TV and went about my business.

I headed to work and after a long and slightly stressful day, returned back to my new king-sized pad. I cooked up dinner but then heard the noise again as the sun went down. It was louder, deeper, actually chilling. The voice from the other tenant was contorted. It almost sounded inhuman. I felt a little creeped out and called my landlord, who assured me he'd contact them to make sure they were okay. I tried my best to sleep that night, though freaked out, because that creeping moan vibrated through the walls.

Then next day I heard it again and decided to take action. I purchased a small gift basket from a shop on the way back to the apartment, something small, just $10, but something to break the ice. The apartment was seriously a dream come true and I wasn't about to let anything bubble into conflict if I could help it. I'd slept so little from the horrible groaning and I was exhausted, so I needed to confront them. I knocked on the door and waited, listening to a slow shuffle to the door, which then creaked open slowly, revealing a sickly, thin man, with hollow cheeks and an open mouth as if frozen mid-sentence. His skin was pale, almost a milky gray, hair thin, and he was wearing a bathrobe that cut down in a V to expose multiple jutting ribs. He looked terrifying and I had to force myself not to gasp at his appearance.

I offered him the basket, explaining I was his new neighbor and wanted to introduce myself. He nodded, staring at me with distant eyes that looked both confused and sad, mouth hanging open the entire time. He was clearly not much of a talker. I just said, "Hi, I'm your new neighbor; pleasure to meet you. Let me know if I can do anything for you; just give me a knock!" and then I turned around, releasing the forced smile on my face into the horrific grimace I'd been holding back.

The man looked like he was on the verge of death, and smelled like it, too. I called the landlord who guaranteed me he'd talk to him. I was exhausted but also starving, and so I headed to the grocery store so I could make some chicken. On the way back I looked around the side of his apartment, glancing through the window to see him eating dinner. "Well, that's a good sign at least," I muttered to myself before heading in to cook. I scarfed down dinner and returned to watching TV when I heard him again. It was the same agonized groaning that chilled my spine. I was in dire need of sleep and cold sweat sent a shiver up my spine. I slept horribly again because the crawling groan was louder, keeping me up, knotting my stomach, and raising every hair on my body in horripilation.

I had no energy from lack of sleep, nodding out at my desk and trying to force myself to walk to my much-needed lunch. I decided to meet another neighbor to ask about the strange tenant, and after an endless work day I picked up another gift basket to present to the person. As I climbed to the second floor (I was on the first), I heard that horrible groan again and I was sure they could hear it from up there as well.

A woman answered, beautiful, but thinner than I expected. She said hello and accepted the basket. She said she'd heard it but had no idea, as she was new just like me. I explained I was losing much needed sleep over it and she advised she had been as well. I thanked her for her time and headed downstairs. I was famished and exhausted and ate the rest of the chicken before lying down as a wave of nausea washed over me. I was sweating profusely, thinking the heater must be on. Old buildings like this had no thermostat so I was stuck for the time being. I was famished so I headed to the grocery store to stock up on ingredients and some steak I was craving. I woke up from that terrible groan again at 2 a.m. and made another snack. My stomach was horribly upset, aching with a throb. I felt like I needed a doctor but it was too late to do anything about it at that particular time.

I called out sick this week. I don't want to work anyways. I am hungry, and the landlord has been kind enough to bring groceries to me, which is helpful, as I'm too sick to make that trek across the street, too sick to talk. I've been starving, ribs poking out and fat shrinking from my tightening body, and he clearly understands that. I don't want to go outside. When the hunger comes I've been groaning myself, and that usually gets his attention unless it's nighttime. He only brings groceries during the day. I feel an insatiable hunger and know it's not mine but my tenant's. The voice is telling me to stay, to eat, as I slowly nod in agreement. The parasitic tenant in my body who found a new apartment when I found mine, drinking a cool glass of water before signing the lease. I haven't heard my neighbor in days; I think his lease is up.

REST STOP

I've been on the road 15 years, and after some long hauls the last few, I was in my very own Peterbilt 379 tractor truck. I was headed north to Boston with a reefer (refrigerated truck) full of slabs of pig, the third trip there in a month. I had a few hours to go and the sun was sinking fast into dusk, and I had to piss something awful. My Jolt bottle was filled and consequently there was no chance I could trucker bomb it. I saw the signs for a rest stop a few miles ahead and figured I could make it. "10-100," I said over the CB radio to Hank, who'd I'd been chatting with. As the rest stop entered my view, my swollen bladder was ready to burst, burning below my belly. The place wasn't much of a rest stop, more of a wooden building in a lawn cut out from the trees. There was no restaurants, gift shop, fuel or anything. It was a wood paneled bathroom, a single street light beaming low and yellow down on it, but the toilet signs were good enough for me. I pushed the brakes and steered my baby into the entrance, parked, and then ran into the bathroom faster than green grass through a goose.

A wave of relief began to wash over me as I began that much-needed emptying. I looked around the older facility; it was pretty dark, and clearly not often frequented, let alone cleaned. Some stall doors were missing, shit was speckled on black plastic lids, and graffiti scratched cursing bedecked the stall doors. It stank something fierce but my god that piss felt good. My eyes followed the dried, splatted flies from previous fists on the yellow tile above the urinal, to the scrawling of phone numbers and dick boasting comments. The high, brown stains near the ceiling I was sure as shit, *was* shit. Over to the foggy light peeking through the cloudy gray of the window I looked and by god I nearly soiled my pants when I saw it.

In the window to my right, behind that foggy, chicken wire glass, was a head, a blurry face on pale, hairless skin facing me, lit by the one overhead light outside. My bladder stopped and I couldn't remove my frozen gaze as the head cocked violently to a diagonal position and lowered out of view.

"Fuck's sake," I thought, hoping it was just a lot lizard looking for a desperate, horny trucker or something. But my heart was beating double time from that fast, unnatural motion it made. I zipped up then reached in my pocket and slid on my knuckle dusters, feeling the weight of the brass as my fingers slid into them. My ear twitched as I heard that god awful sound. It was like a baby crying mixed with a balloon being squeezed slowly while pinching the lips. My neck hairs stood to the sky and I turned to the bathroom entrance where the sound came from. I watched a long shadow grow on that filthy, brown metal door, too fuzzy to make out anything except that it was long. I'm no chicken, have been in plenty of fights and am built solid, but I was scared as a long-tailed cat in a room full of rockers at that damned wheezing, crying sound. There was something about that noise I was certain no human being should or even could possibly make.

I slapped my brass knuckles on my open palm and boomed, "Whoever is out there better haul ass fast 'cause my pistol don't miss!" I saw the shadow on the door become darker, as whoever or whatever approached, and I stepped into that filthy stall, peering out the door. The pale man's head entered my view from outside at an impossible angle. From the top right corner of the door frame, upside down, the bald white face leaned in. It then slithered all the way inside to the floor, revealing a thin, hairy neck with three joints, long, long segments like a giraffe's leg, with a foot lodged in the base of the skull. This ... leg, was reaching in from the outside, from the top of the door to the floor, to the severed head surrounding the unseen foot like a boot, now pressed top down on piss-filled tiles. The upside down face stared, silent and dead.

The head stank of rot bad enough to gag a maggot and so I covered my mouth with the crook of my flannel-covered elbow. The long, deer-like limb crunched in a violent twist upward, swiveling the rotting severed head to an upright position. It was then that I saw how stretched the limb attached to it was, like the skin on a deer was covering something else, too big for its britches. The mouth on that pasty corpses' head was motionless but let out that awful sound, a high pitched squeal of wheezing that froze my blood. The long leg cracked as another impossible joint formed from splitting bone, echoing off the filthy walls with a sickening crunch, and the limb reached further into the bathroom.

I doubted those dead eyes on that detached head could see, but I fully retreated into the stall and waited. I swear, it was as if something unnatural, something massive, crawled into a deer, and was trying to lure me out using the familiar face of my own kind. It was like bait on a line, and that rot infested head was supposed to be a tasty worm. I slowly closed the stall door and locked it, very aware of the large gaps above the chicken scrawl graffiti and dried shit on the dividers. There was another horrible cracking sound of bone snapping as the head popped up above the stall door in front of me, and I swear, if I didn't just relieve myself, my jeans would have been soaked through. I held my breath and stared, and waited, frozen as dread poured through my sweaty body.

I used to swim by Mr. Miller's pond as a kid, and I'd heard of the brain eating amoeba that took Sarah's life that summer, turning her head into a pig trough for the little parasitic buggers. By the time they realized she was seriously sick she dropped dead, brain dissolved and chewed up like a juicy orange by a hungry horse. I remembered that story whenever swimming at Mr. Millers' place, and I learned how to hold my breath for longer than anybody my age out of fear of catching any of those deadly parasites. I'd like to tip my cap to the unfortunate Sarah now as I reckon I owe her my life.

I sat in that stall, breath locked in my lungs, and waited out the horrific squeal that thing made, the other sounds of snapping bone under the hijacked corpse, the eventual shadow on the ceiling retreating out the door and into the night. Whether bored, confused or onto another meal elsewhere, that godless horror exited, leaving me in that pisser alone. I breathed in deeply, as I was starved of oxygen, and likely blue in the face. I waited a few minutes before sneaking gently and cautiously back to my rig. I've never been happier to see her. I started her up, peeled out and hammered down, hitting the fast lane like a bat out of hell, eyes fixed on the rear view.

With only one hour to Boston to go then, I swear if I didn't need to piss again, but I was letting it go in my jeans. I picked up the radio, telling Hank I had a hell of a story for him, and tried to relax in my seat. I caught a glimpse of myself in the rear view and I looked like ten miles of bad road, pale skin and eyes stuck wide. I'm still stiff as a board and my heart won't stop hammering in my chest. I know it's got to be my imagination but I swore at the last light, as I slowed to a halt I heard a buzzing cry from behind me ... from my trailer.

THE RESCUE

My entire life I've loved dogs. If the eyes are windows to the soul, a dog's windows have no blinds, unlike those of man. They don't hide emotion or cower behind a false pretense; they live honestly and love unconditionally, and I knew since I was eight that I wanted to work with them. After graduating high school, I finally achieved my goal when searching for a summer job. I covered my bases by applying at a number of restaurants, retail positions and theaters, but my heart was set on the vet, the animal rescue or possibly dog walking. I was pleasantly surprised when I got an email back to set up an interview with a local vet. They needed a kennel assistant and I was very happy to accept when I aced the interview and was offered the job.

It was straightforward and simple: clean the mess, feed and water them, shampoo and dry them, then walk them at noon and 3 p.m., and finally feed and water then lock them up each night. Nail trimming and check-ups would come later after the holidays. I was thrilled to work with the furry friends, helping the lives of the little animals with purrs and cuddles enriching every day. I didn't even mind cleaning up their waste, as I was truly content. That changed a few days ago when an unnamed dog was brought in.

For the past week the job had been a dream, aside from the 7:30 a.m. sign in (I'm no morning person), and 5:00 p.m. clock out. I was making due, however, and until that mutt came in I was more than happy to make adjustments. It was an exercise in self-restraint and commitment. Wednesday, however, I saw the truck pull in and my co-worker exited the vehicle before heading to the back of the truck. He re-entered my view leading a large, black mess of clotted hair on a leash pole, keeping his distance. The breed was unidentifiable, but it was very tall, taller than a Great Dane and the putrid stink hit me before the thing was less than five meters from me. It filled the space with an odorous wave of shit and piss build-up of the most unhygienic and uncared-for homeless person, and a gamy smell added to the tangy, putrid mix that made it far worse. As it drew closer, my eyes widened and my throat closed up in shock; it was missing its lower jaw completely, a horrific row of fangs unending in the void of gore and fur below. It sent chills into my spine I'd not previously felt.

"They'll prolly put it down, tomorrow most likely," the driver, Corey, said with clear pity in his voice. "It's been on a chain for at least three years. The owner might be going to jail, at least." He shook his head low, and I noted he loved animals as much as I did and had been there for nearly a year. I slowly approached and petted the neglected creature's head, trying not to focus on the long, purple tongue hanging down like a flesh necktie over dreadlocked, clumped black hair and that rotted wound of a maw. I felt something writhing and turned my palm upward to reveal a few squirming maggots on my now brown-smeared hand. It stared at me with harrowing, milky eyes that did not belong on a living beast. I bolted to the metal sink, vomiting into it and blanching my hand with hot water. Corey laughed nervously, bringing the dog to the cleaning station as I tried to recover. I looked up with unease and noticed the protruding spine beneath the animal's matted back fur, heaving with bassy, gasping breaths.

It looked off, like the proportions of its jointed leg sections were too long or perhaps too many. It walked in slow, with stalking movements that almost implied a hunter's instinct. The thing freaked me out as it didn't even look like any breed I'd ever seen. When Casey returned from the washing area, it looked more or less the same, and the awful stench of it was slightly reduced. Corey said he needed help cutting clotted hair so I agreed to assist.

He held the massive beast with the pole collar and I felt the thick dreaded fur to make sure it was actually fur as I sheared into it. The matted dreads were dense, tiny bugs weaved in and out, maggots as well, and each cut chunk released fouler, unimaginable odors. I knew the dog would just be put down regardless, and this was horrifically disgusting, but I kept clipping away and doing my best to clean it.

By the time we removed the major bulk of crusty flaps of dreads, I'd been working an hour overtime, and the hound was slowly wagging its newly freed tail. We shampooed and deloused it again, fed it some formula I gave her, the gender now visible through dense fur and scabbed, dried skin, a soft petting on the head. I was relieved to see no maggots this time around. She actually stank far less. I washed up, helped lock up, and got in the car to drive home. In the parking lot, as I unlocked my car door, however, I heard a shuffling sound that froze my heart. I spun around and saw nothing, but I hurried inside and locked the doors. *This day couldn't get creepier*, I thought. I was horribly wrong. I couldn't get the terrifying image of the beast out of my head.

I was on the highway when the high beams flashed behind me. I slowed to let them pass, but they just slowed as well. I gave them ample time to pass, but whomever it was lurked behind, eventually hanging back until out of view. I shook it off and got off my exit and spotted the truck in my rear view again, taking the same exit. Just then I felt a faint gust of hot, damp breath on my neck. I shouted in terror, startled, nearly crashing into the barrier, and screeched my car to a halt. I bolted out of the door and backed away in terror on the side of the road, looking in the backseat but seeing nothing. The truck slowed to a stop behind me, high beams blinding, and the door opened; the silhouette of a large man exited the vehicle.

"There's s-something in my car, I think… " I stuttered, panic flooding my rapid pulsing blood. I didn't realize it then but I was in shock. A man approached and I saw his wrinkled, angry brow and snarling, red head over dirty overalls and ripped jeans. Grey stubble and sneering hatred was etched into the 50 something's face. "You fucks took my dog, my fucking property," he bellowed loudly, his voice deep and shaky with anger. I then noticed the heavy, rusted wrench in his right fist. I saw his arm swing and I fell sideways to the ground. My head was wet. I touched my pulsating temple and my hand pulled away, red with blood. I lifted my hands to block the next strike, which shattered my wrist with unbearable pain. I looked up to beg for my life, to explain we were rescuing an animal in need, to express my anger at him for abusing a life worth far more than his. I was going to die on that road, though, and I knew it. When the black, clumped tangles of fur rose behind him, however, the blows stopped.

It stood easily a foot over his head, the gaping, mutilated mouth under furrowed canine brows entombing the horrible glossy blank eyes. The long fangs hammered down with a sickening crunch on the top of his head and blood spouted upward in crimson arcs. The black, clumpy beast this man was attacking me to steal back, scraped mounds of flesh from his face in violent, downward hammering. It was upright on its long, quivering hind legs, plowing down into the growing cavity of gore spewing from the skull. The nose and mouth were crushed and gouged until brains dropped from the crater where they once existed. When it was finished, the hollowed head was beyond recognition. The unnamed rescue sat and stared at me with the haunting eyes no animal should possess.

I named her Adder. I feed her formula daily. I can't pet her much, because she doesn't seem to like being touched. I did what I could in terms of dressing her wounds from frostbite, infections, and her missing jaw, which was not enough to hide the jarring terror of her entire being. She will never look or even behave like any normal dog ever should. When I take her out, parents cover their children's eyes and grown men cross the street with abject fear. Dogs whimper and run without a single bark; they run as far as they possibly can when she is near. Dog parks would simply be evil so I walk her at night in barren areas.

She haunts my nights as well, staring at me with those insane eyes, sometimes upright and tall on shaky hind legs at the foot of my bed before I can eventually fall asleep. I occasionally enjoy having a loyal pet so formidable and nightmarish that nobody alive would ever try to bother me while walking her. It's the least I can do for this companion I owe my life to, Adder, who somehow slipped out of the shelter, into my car, and rescued me.

THE SMEAR AT 10:32

It started after my parents left for dinner. I'd declined the offer to join, hoping to catch up on some college assignments, but I ended up skipping them completely and they were really the furthest thing from my mind. There was an emergency alert on my phone, something I rarely find myself concerned with, but this one had me curious. I had been sitting in my old bedroom I used to live in prior to college, about to conduct some research, when a jarring vibration shook the desk I'd used as a teen. The text simply read:

EMERGENCY ALERT
Hostile animal this area 10:32. PM EST Tue. Avoid Wooded Areas. Check media. Type: Severe

I found this one intriguing indeed. Was there a bear on the loose or possibly an exotic pet that got free? I'd known of some kids in the city who raised alligators, but in my parents' woods there were nothing but deer, squirrels and an occasional rabbit; no bears or carnivores of any size lived around here. I didn't think much of it, but the woods were always a bit too dark for my liking, hence the reason I'd chosen the city when choosing my college.

By the way, my parent's house has an abundance of windows. They love light, and I am sure this was their reason for moving here when we were all younger. I walked to my window and peered out into the dark evening, observing the barely visible trees shrouded in shadow. A few moths gathered in front of the windowpane but nothing was out there, at least from my angle. For some reason I felt a bit anxious, so I walked over and turned the porch light on to increase visibility, just in case. I headed into the kitchen to refill my water glass, contemplating a sip of whiskey from the liquor shelf, but changed my mind.

I then walked over to the front door, next to those two large windows that extended nearly to door height and turned on the walkway lights. I felt some comfort and walked back to the kitchen when I saw something moving in the woods, which started about 10 meters from the sliding kitchen door. I was fairly sure my mind was likely playing tricks on me, but I stared into the edge of the woods and was sure I saw movement, slow and awkward. My heart skipped a beat as I turned on the outside light that illuminated the view from the kitchen-side door.

At the edge of the woods I saw a barely lit animal. It took me a few seconds to register. It was a deer but its abdomen looked far too long. It was shivering, or more accurately, lurching in a stagger on swaying stalks of legs. Its white eyes reflecting the light were too far apart as well, and I realized as it turned its head that the eyes seemed nearly two feet apart. The other eye that came into view was nearly half of a foot wide as well, an oblong reflector that smeared across its wide, unnatural head. Shivers rippled across my neck as I watched it lift and drop the massive, deformed head in effort and release, as if unaccustomed to its current state.

I figured I'd send my parents a text but noticed it wasn't going through, just hanging on "delivering". I then saw my phone service was on zero bars, which was bizarre, as I'd texted a friend not 20 minutes before. I checked the internet, and when I realized that was down, I began to worry. I walked over to the television and turned it on, flipping to the local channels where an anchorman glitched and paused as the signal struggled. There was a news ticker on the bottom displaying an alert of massive power outages, and I felt great relief that my electricity had not been affected. I could make out some of the dialogue in between broken words, and what I gathered was that there were numerous animal attacks andI swear he was saying, "unexplained deformations".

Occasionally the anchorman's image would blend in the style of a weak signal to confusing photographs, photographs that took me a few moments to realize were wide, gnarled trees, power lines that tapered into extensive mammoth ropes, and dead cattle that were appallingly bloated and pulled, which appeared to have been tampered heavily with a photo editing tool. They were all stretched unnaturally, as if the objects were fresh oil paintings that someone had smeared quite hard with the palm of their hand. It looked Dali-esque, and as much as I appreciated Dali's art, the images on screen horrified me. I watched for a few minutes and realized the station was trying to piece things together as well. The pixelated anchorman froze in place before the "signal lost" message appeared on screen.

I walked back to the kitchen door, relieved to see no sign of the deer, and pulled a butcher knife from the drawer. I slipped my boots on and walked to the front of the house which faces our neighbor's yard, and peered over at the light of their window. It was no longer the shape I'd seen each night as a teenager. It was a long, wavy band of yellow, barely visible beyond the pear trees which separated us. I stared at it for a few seconds in awe and then let out a short shout of terror as I saw the figure staggering out from under the tree.

It was so horribly altered that I couldn't tell if it was Mr. or Mrs. Daniels, a wide head with strands of grey, ribbon hair dangling over the wide slits of nostrils and hot dog shaped, watery, white eyes. The mouth was a massive hanging horror on the jaws, burdening the bent neck with its current weight. The figure was approaching my house in slow, labored staggers, and I stared jaw agape for a few seconds before I could force myself to look away. I checked my phone again, dialing 911 immediately after seeing one bar flickering on and off. I received a busy signal before the call ended prematurely. Signal lost.

I opened the front door, ready to call out to the figures to see if they were still themselves, but immediately heard the low, vibratory screaming, inhuman and choked by whatever caused the face and vocal cords to stretch. I shut the door and locked it, and abruptly turned off the living room light and watched from around the corner. As it walked into the spot lighting of our exterior lights, I saw the twisted face and massive chest, the enormous left leg and the widened nails on the impossibly fat fingers on what was once a normal arm. It was Mrs. Daniels; she walked straight into the long window I now resented my parents for choosing, with a clink of a fat tooth, smearing an absurd amount of saliva on the glass as she wiped her open mouth on it. Her brain had to have been equally deformed, and though not dead, there was nothing I could do for her.

The thud from the kitchen door nearly collapsed me; I spun violently to see an elongated deer, at first thinking it was the same one I'd seen earlier but soon realizing it wasn't. It was deformed as if diagonally, a massive tongue drooping out of the horrific, toothy mouth onto the back porch, and one massive antler weighing its cocked heavy head low to the ground. I ran to my room and grabbed my computer and chargers, a comforter and pillow. I tried not to look at the awful things in the harsh spot lighting, smearing their horrific heads on the windows on either side of the house. I stalled at the television, which had a frozen photo of a jet immersed in the shock wave of the sound barrier being broken, wondering if it was related to the horror unfolding around me, when the loud bang on the living room window left me reeling in agony. I raced to the most interior room of the house by instinct, the pantry which had no windows.

There was a washer and dryer which I switched off, in order to better hear. I've been in here a while now, in pitch blackness aside from the dim glow of my computer and phone, and I don't expect to move anytime soon. The bathroom is connected to this room, but I'm not sure it's locked and I'll wait until desperate to check. In the meantime I've been using the utility sink. It's 11:15 now. I was able to send an email to my parents and friends but received none back. I only assume it will pass, and I've been making sure to keep silent, but I can't stop shaking after hearing the shattering of windows.

There were sounds of scraping limbs all night long and I heard a loud sniffing from the crack under the door on a few occasions. More broken glass was scattering under unseen feet. A few times through the course of the night the television signal strengthened. I heard the anchorman's voice, stressing to stay indoors, mentioning an anonymous caller with possible insight, rumors of an experimental military aircraft, and something about molecular vibration in between the sound clipping out. I still have no phone service and my parents never returned home. The sunlight has been peeking under the door for a few hours now, but I still hear them. I hear their low, agonized screams, deep and rippled with the vibration of fattened vocal chords. There are bands of moving shadows under the thin, wooden door protecting me, the door that has a hole from where a distorted antler punched through last night as I squeezed my knees to my chest, holding my breath. As I type this, I'm shaking, trying not to rattle the laptop. Through the hole I can see an eye rolling in its socket as if trying to process what it is seeing. I think it is Mrs. Daniels.

Everything became worse. That evening I heard less motion from outside the door. I gripped the knife and picked up a trash can lid as a makeshift shield. I readied for an attack and slowly cracked the door to the evening's darkness, the TV flashing "signal lost" to light the room, and a breeze dancing in the drapes over shattered windows, which covered the floor. I walked over to the front of the house and saw the backlit figure standing by the shattered window, facing outward. I immediately thought of Mrs. Daniels and her terrifying face, but God, when it turned around ... it was my mother. She turned and tried to speak out of that wide streak of a mouth across her disfigured, bulging head. "Wha-wha-wh-what's what's wrooooooong wi-wi-with muh muh me?" she asked with horrific and widely stretched eyes. Her arms began lashing quickly and violently forward as if eager to reach me, to rip at me.

"Mom, I am going to get help. Stay here" I pleaded, trying not to allow the terror in my body to enter my voice as she approached on wobbling, bowed legs arced out to one side. Her rapidly swinging, grabbing arms were close and I had to step back in order to avoid them. She just repeated that phrase over and over in muffled slow stutters that brought tears to my eyes and chills to my spine. I then noticed the bloody handprints on her navy blue fleece. A man's prints. My father's prints. I ran. She chased but I was faster. I leapt out a tall door of a window and into the long driveway and saw them, heads low, staring with deformed faces from the woods edge. There were dozens of deer, possibly other creatures or dogs as well. It was difficult to identify their species in the lumpy, elongated misshapen bodies, and massive eyes and jaws. I ran into the black, winding street, shadows engulfing it aside from the fog of low red from the tail lights of the warped car, past the driver's side window stretched out in a rippling deformity where my mother had been sitting at the time of whatever this was happened. My father's faceless corpse was still belted behind the wheel, absolute terror in the exposed eyeballs and jaw frozen mid-scream.

I ran past dozens of driveways and saw no lights on. Howls and tortured, vibrating screams called out from the shadows. I heard a rumble and saw the growing amber of headlights approaching. I tried to wave the vehicle down but it didn't slow. I dove into the ditch on the side of the road, narrowly avoiding being hit. The truck was clearly military, covered in that familiar dull green. I ran until I got to the nearest store a mile out. It was completely empty but I found the back door unlocked. Finally I was able to breathe, collapsing onto the floor before panting heavily. I broke down in tears. I did find a computer in the back office and a generator. I had to kill the lights, however, as it attracted the dogs, or what once were dogs, their massive, sharp, skewed teeth flickering in the moonlight as they swayed in front of the shop window at me, staring.

There must be at least six of them, mouths like crocodiles and white eyes that can only process what to use them on. They are nearly eight feet in length and they look ravenous. One is wiping a gnarled set of massive teeth on the bubbled in window, another twitching on mangled legs, its head dragging. I followed the smeared tiles, bleeding backward across the store through rippled junk foods and long jars of condiments, peanut butters and olive oils looking like abstract sculptures, to the storage room and its concave, bulging door where from the other side I heard a bassy groan. The door handle jiggles but it's locked from the other side, out of my control. I'm just praying whoever is in there has a mind that is too far gone to figure it out.

Not sure if any of the emails are getting out, as I have received nothing yet, just emailing everybody in hopes they are alive, possibly to send help. I used the baseball bat behind the register on one of the dogs that chased me as I ran. Most were too deformed to run anymore, but one was even faster, it was on me in moments. My arm is bleeding badly from the terrible jaws of that thing, but not bleeding as badly as its crushed head. It stings horribly and I used my belt to make a tourniquet. I couldn't afford to pass out with the sun nearly down.

I made it to a house with power and a second story. I checked the rooms and I think I'm finally alone. There's plenty of food in the fridge and cabinets to last me a while, but I have no idea whether to stay put and call attention to the house for possible help or not. Something about the way that military truck was driving straight into me makes me fearful. I may try to put a message on the roof with lights and sheets, but I'm not trying to make myself known yet. And once I saw what happened to the birds around here, I don't want anything to do with that roof.

I finally found a car with keys. During my second day at the house I heard the trucks, a long line of them that were slowly driving down the street, putting bullets and fire in everything moving. One by one they torched houses and I barely got out before they saw me. I bolted across the back lawn into a housing development and finally found an old, unlocked Camry with keys in the change holder. I drove until I saw roadblocks in the distance then changed my course over and over. I've been using some binoculars I found in a house full of mutilated bodies, likely a family. After finding an unblocked dirt road out of town, I've been driving for two hours. I've passed other cars now. The radio works out here. I listen to news radio mentioning the fire in my town. It was a perfect storm of a brush fire they said, all the weather and winds creating the horrible destruction of the small town's forests and the tragic loss of life. I'm off to the city to figure out how to return to my life and address the loss, and how to make sure this story is told.

SOMETHING TRAPPED ME IN THE BATHROOM STALL TODAY

I work in an office building where the entire floor shares the men and women's bathrooms. I've been here a year and am familiar with a few people on the floor, but I am not the kind of guy to try and engage in small talk while in an embarrassing position. Anyways, today I had to use the facilities and entered the bathroom, then a stall in the back. As I was finishing up, the door opened slowly, then shut with a jarring bang. I was startled, but just sat on the seat, waiting for the person to hurry and exit so I could wash my hands and return back to the office. No sounds were coming, and the person clearly wasn't using the sink or the toilet. I wondered if he turned back to get something or to make a phone call and left, but I lowered my head to the bottom gap between the floor and saw dress shoes pointed directly at the stall where I sat.

I was a bit creeped out, but I wasn't letting this person wait me out. One thing I hated was people seeing me emerge from a toilet. Don't ask me why, I just don't personally like to be identified as "that person". Another thing I hated was being rushed. I sat there for a few minutes, still hearing no sound, and checked my phone, ripped toilet paper and flushed it. Nothing. I looked back under and stared at those shiny leather shoes under dark dress pants just pointing at me. What the hell was this asshole doing?

I coughed loudly to signal to the lurking man he was being rude. I waited a few minutes, realizing I had to get back to work, and simply had to deal with walking by this jerk. I was about to open the stall door when it shook from a loud, booming pound. I yelped in fright and shouted, "Fuck! What the hell?!" There was no response, then I heard some horrible gurgling sounds from the other side that sounded awful and inhuman. I was truly scared at this point, heart racing, and I peered down to the gap near the floor once more to see the shoes directly in front of the stall I sat in.

"Please give me some space, sir," I stated, trying not to sound as nervous as I was. No response. I said, "fuck it" and stood upright and fastened my belt. I turned the lock and started to push the door open but couldn't budge it. The man clearly was forcing it shut with all his weight. "Get away from the door or I'm calling the cops," I said firmly, seriously dreading any confrontation with the guy. I heard some whispered panting that truly unnerved me, followed by a horrible, saliva-filled grunt.

"MOVE!" I ordered, shaking the door, but the man didn't budge. He just stood there, holding the stall door closed. At this point I was horrified. I was in the least trafficked office bathroom I ever worked with, and since we shared one key for the office I knew no coworkers would be in until I returned with it. In desperation, I loudly stated, "I'm calling 911," and as if in response I saw clear fluid drip to the floor near the stall entrance, repulsing me. I was horrified, realizing it was probably saliva and nothing worse, but was seriously disgusted and afraid.

Out of options aside from driving my weight into the stall door, I dialed 911. I spoke loudly so the man could hear as I stated the emergency and gave the address. The minutes that followed felt like an eternity. Horrible, disgusting and inhuman sounds buzzed from the other side of the stall, as if the man was trying to get as close as possible with the barrier in the way. More splashing, clear liquid spattered on the tile floor, then a pool of yellow began to trail into view from beyond the metal walls confining me.

Eventually there was a banging on the bathroom door to the outside hall, the announcement that the police were there and to open up. I waited what felt like an hour until they finally returned with a key.

"Jesus Christ," I heard an officer say, soles of shoes shuffling and slapping in a jog on the tile just out of view. I opened the door slowly, realizing it was finally unobstructed. "Heart attack, looks like," the officer said, and then I stared down at the body of the overweight man in an expensive suit, with a blue face and bloodshot eyes. His mouth was dripping with drool and pants wet, the dead, staring eyes on the lifeless corpse of the man that died standing before falling into the stall door, forcing it shut.

THE WRITHING THING FROM THE WOODS

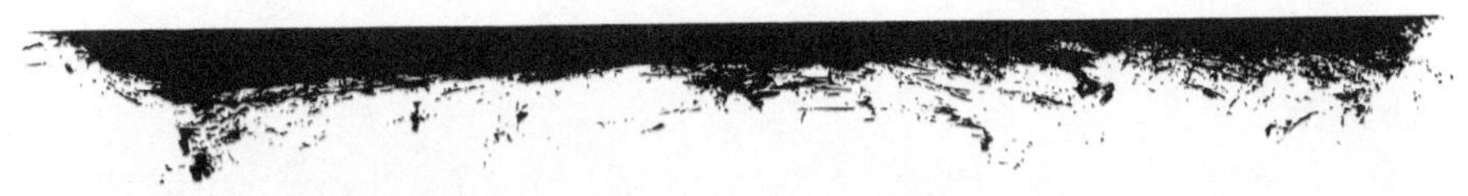

I was in my parents' kitchen chopping onions as my mother had requested, to help out with dinner that evening. I had stopped by on my way back to college after enjoying a wonderful time travelling abroad for volunteer work. I was just getting back into school mode, picking the archaeology and anthropology classes I thought would best prepare me for the field. My eyes began to water from the onion, as they always do, so I took a break and walked to the large glass window, opening it for some fresh air when I saw it.

Quivering in the distance above the tree line of the woods, something enormous stood writhing or twitching. It was massive and elongated, likely 60 feet high. I couldn't make it out clearly as it was quite a ways back and blurry (and I'm a bit near-sighted). It was out of place and eerie, but unable to comprehend what exactly I was looking at, I eventually returned to helping with the dinner preparation, onion tears and all. When I looked out the window again it was gone.

The next morning I returned to the kitchen window once more out of curiosity and saw the thing yet again, waving in an unnatural motion, flailing and massive. I jolted in horror, letting out a gasp of terror and dropped the cereal bowl I was holding to the floor, cascading milk and flakes across the linoleum. "What the hell!" my dad shouted, and I told him to come check it out. "I'm busy; what is it?" he asked, clearly annoyed.

"There's ... something out in the woods," I replied as he trudged downstairs.

He squinted and spat. "What? Where?"

I looked out, and just like a frustrating movie moment, it was gone.

"I'm not crazy; there was something out there, something large, and it's taller than the trees." I tried to explain, knowing I sounded like a fool. He just laughed, made a snarky comment I'd rather omit, and made a sandwich while I tried to understand the thing I had seen.

That evening when the sun had set I turned on the front lights of the house, blinded by the brightness for a moment before seeing it again, twitching violently at the front of the woods, far closer, maybe 20 meters away. I shouted with shock, and stared at that ... thing that looked like a giant, undulating nerve-shaped worm maybe 60 feet high, writhing at the forest edge in front of the trees. It was standing vertically, branching out into short, quivering stalks at the top, tiny amorphous arms that stretched slowly in all directions. I had no idea what to do but instinctively pulled my phone from my pocket with shivering hands and pointed the camera at it. When I looked up I saw it was gone, likely back into the woods out of view, and I was more than frustrated. I knew what I had seen; it was not a hallucination or my imagination. It was as if the thing was stalking me, then hiding, and it was getting closer.

I had a hard time passing out that night. Nightmares of that tall, worm-like creature horrified my sweat soaked sleep. I jolted awake at 4:30 a.m. and shuffled to the bathroom to refill my cup of water. I turned on the light and facing the mirror I screamed. Directly in front of me, inside the bathroom, was a 9 foot tall writing black thing, twitching in place. I collapsed backwards, crawling back on my elbows, reeling with terror, staring at the horrific, inhuman thing as it followed me, closing in. I couldn't stop screaming and I felt everything slow and blur. My heart felt like it stopped beating from utter horror and my mind screamed with unimaginable, maddening trauma. I turned away, clawing at the carpet, unable to breathe through my grimacing, open mouth. I felt it seize me and I cringed and screamed louder before losing consciousness.

A moment later my blurry eyes focused on the face of my father. I was dizzy and exhausted, my body depleted from shock, and my lungs were struggling to breathe. He said he left his bedroom to see me crawling and screaming, but nothing was there, only me. He explained he had grabbed my arm and I passed out. He made an emergency appointment with our family physician the next day. I didn't sleep. I just lay in bed, unable to close my eyes. I was in no shape for any nightmares as I was already living in one. I began to realize I might actually be going insane for the first time.

The next day we drove into the cluster of medical offices and entered to sign paperwork and meet the doctor. I just knew the he was going to recommend seeing a psychiatrist, but as I sat in his sterile office on the paper covered table answering questions, he grabbed an ophthalmoscope, blindingly bright as he began examining my eyes. Upon doing so I clawed back in horror as that writhing thing stood in the office. "Aha," he said, which startled me in relief as I wasn't crazy; he'd seen something. "It's a type of Loa Loa, a parasitic worm that can infect the eye. You must've contracted it in the woods when volunteering in Sierra Leone. It likely took a moment to hide when exposed to bright lights, which..."

"Get it out! Get it out! God, please get it out!" I pleaded, trying not to lose myself to madness. He set up a medication regimen as well as a surgery the following day to remove the large adult worm or worms, I chose not to learn which, from my eye ...

OUR DOG PULLED SOMETHING FROM THE SEA

We took our last family trip to Cape Cod to help Dad clean the place and enjoy some nature for a few days, despite the drop in temperature. It was nearly pitch black outside when the house came into view. My sister and I had gotten on each other's nerves in the back seat after a bit, so I had been playing some games on my phone to pass the time during the long ride before arriving. We had been driving for hours and I was relieved to finally stretch my clenched legs out of the car and into the cold night's air.

Tucker sprang over us from the back, knocking the phone out of my hand, which led me to blurt out a profanity before getting reprimanded by my father. Tucker was energetic for his old age, which showed in his greying snout and foggy eyes. He was a decent sized Weimaraner I'd known over half my life, an excellent companion through walks and adventures, and I loved him despite his clumsiness. He bolted out to the water immediately and Dad told me to get him as he unloaded our stuff with my mom and sister.

I followed the unlit path in the reeds, just wishing to be inside and out of the cold. I bellowed his name into the night and followed his tracks down the embankment. "Tucker!! Come!" I kept calling, walking beyond the tall grass and into the sand, seeing some motion near the lapping waves at the water's edge. There was a surprising amount of algae on the beach and a number of dead fish, too. It looked like a peculiar scene. I swear it was almost as if everything from the sea was suddenly desperate to leave. I saw Tucker up to his chest in water, tugging a large black object form below the murky waves, rippling his back muscles. I began feeling a bit nervous as I approached and saw he was tugging something rather large and similar in color to the black seaweed strewn across the shore from the waves.

When I reached him he yelped and let go of whatever he'd been tugging on. The object sank back into the water before I could see it. I was about to call him when he whimpered then ran quickly to me and burrowed his wet head between my legs, shivering. I gave him a pat and led him inside, looking back into the dark water but seeing nothing. Whatever he had a hold of appeared to be gone. I was a bit on edge at the site of all of the dead clams, starfish, crabs and other sea critters, as this wasn't too uncommon, just not to that extent.

Mom made a simple pasta dinner and we ate the meal while talking about possible colleges once I graduated the following summer. Dinner was fine and we had a few laughs, looking forward to the weekend, until I noticed Tucker whimpering and scooting on the tile floor in the mudroom. My family looked over as well, conversation on pause. My sister and I burst out in laughter but we tapered off as humor turned to worry when we saw the black, inky stain that trailed behind him on the carpet. My father stood up in a hurry and rushed over as we watched, disconcerted at the state of our furry friend, and rubbed Tucker's soggy head. "What's wrong with him? He was yanking on something in the water ... did he get hurt?" I asked as my father checked him out.

"He seems fine, probably swallowed saltwater. It makes dogs sick," my father explained with a dour frown. The rest of the dinner was a bit quiet, our eyes ever looking at the family dog and that slick, black streak with worry.

After dinner as I washed dishes, I watched Tucker rise from his nap and slowly stalk his way to the bay window, gazing outside with raised hackles, growling. I looked out into the night enveloping the house, wishing we had more lights. I stared into the fuzzy blackness too dense to see into when I heard a jarring sound of three loud knocks. I looked around, realizing my parents had retired to their room. I walked over and yelled, "Someone's here. Answer the door!" and returned to the living room. No response came from them. I continued, "Mom! Dad!" and my little sister looked up from her tablet screen with worried, wide eyes. I walked over and opened the door to their bedroom to find them gone, then I noticed the window curtain dancing in the wind from the open window.

At this point I was genuinely concerned and a bit afraid, so I returned to the living room to get Tucker to help me investigate when I saw the state he was in. He was visibly shivering, eyes wild and intense, staring at me from the shadows of the open closet. I called him but he refused to come out, and when I reached for his collar he whimpered while snapping at me, something I had never seen him do in my life. He coiled deep into the closet corner as the loud sound rang out three times, and I realized it sounded like it was actually coming from outside the door, not the door itself. I approached the window and peered out at the shore.

My eyes widened as I saw my mother just beyond the reeds facing the ocean. A bit worried, I told my sister to stay put and to look after Tucker. I walked outside into the darkness and followed the path down to the sea. My mother was standing in front of a large wooden chest that was damp and black with seaweed. It looked ancient. It was maybe four feet long, and three feet high, and wide with rusty metal accents, barnacles freckling its seaweed strewn exterior.

"Mom?" I called to her, but I received no reaction. She just stood there with her back to me and I just wanted everything to be normal. I wanted to go inside and get my sister and leave, but I didn't. I kept walking towards her, among the dozens of crabs, fish, algae and jellyfish dead in piles at my feet on that long, dark beach.

"Mom?" I begged to her, my eyes locked on that ancient and arcane chest, "Where's Dad?" I realized then she was shivering in the cold of the night. I didn't want to get any closer. I didn't want to see my mom's face, and when that heavy lid slowly opened on its own, something in the recesses of my mind screamed for me to run. I just stood horrified as the lid opened and my mother peered inside as if in a trance. I saw a thick, black silhouetted tendril or arm pushing the lid from the inside and my jaw dropped wide in horror as it rapidly curled around my mother's neck and pulled her into that box with horrific strength and speed. She vanished into the shadowed interior and the lid slammed closed, followed by three loud, horrific crunches I'd mistaken for knocking earlier.

The crunches of the rapidly folding human body had clearly been my dad. I ran in terror to the house, inside to my sister's side and called the police. I locked the doors and windows and waited for an eternity until they arrived. I broke down in tears explaining what had happened to the unbelieving looks on the faces of questioning officers. I led them to the shore, to the dead life that had tried to escape the horrors from the sea, to the drag marks in the sand leading back into the ocean, no chest in sight.

The past month has weighed heavy on my sister and me. The beach was combed thoroughly by rescue crews to no avail and eventually we were informed that we'd be likely be waiting seven years before our parents were declared dead in absentia. My sister and I have been staying at my grandparent's house, and we have been trying to adjust to the new life and move on. Tucker is still ... wrong, but my grandparents just keep explaining dogs change in old age. I see him move with a strange tic and that occasional whimpering scoot on the carpet. It's as if he is trying to get something off of or out of him, some piece of whatever he pulled from that chest in the water, the thing that just stopped my heart mid-beat with horror icing over me as the sounds hammered into my mind, those three cracking sounds from downstairs I know it isn't knocking at the door.

SUBWAY CREEP

I heard the dreaded "Doors are closing" and sprinted to the closest subway car as the doors slid shut, slipping in at the last possible second. I was running late to my job interview due to my phone deciding to freeze and the alarm not functioning; just my luck. Finally on the subway, I panted, hands on my ironed khakis and head low, trying to catch my breath. I'm not overweight, but let's say I could use more exercise and am not used to running. When I lifted my head I saw the car was totally empty, aside from a large, seated man staring at me with awful wide eyes, clearly pleasuring himself.

I darted my eyes away with shock as soon as I realized what I had seen. I felt disgusted and had to force myself not to retch. I heard the disgusting squishing sound but forced myself not to look. It was vile. I'd heard of this type of behavior before but had never witnessed it and was hoping never to have to again. I assured myself that we'd soon be at the next stop, whereupon I'd rush to the next car. Almost as in reaction to that thought, the car braked with a jolt that forced me into a pole and closer to the sick individual. The lights flickered and the last thing I wanted to hear declared, "Ladies and gentlemen, we are being held momentarily." Now closer, I was unable to stop my glance back to the seated, masturbating man in front of me.

He looked to be in his late 50s, gaunt, bald and dirty with grease, most likely homeless. An unkempt moustache curled over his open mouth and messy row of yellowed teeth. He was groaning an awful creaking noise, hand moving back and forth. I intentionally did not look at his private area, only his eyes, as I readied myself to yell at the pervert with enough conviction to reprimand him properly, but I saw something dropping to the floor at his feet and couldn't stop myself from looking. There were drops of crimson spilling down from the jerking man's grimy hands into the growing pool glossing the floor and clinging to the edges of his filthy, lace-less shoes.

I looked back at the pool of blood and upward to his crotch, realizing now it wasn't a sexual organ in his hand but the hilt of a knife. He was plunging the blade repeatedly into his groin, which looked a bloody mangled mess that snapped any possibility I had to keep it together at that point. I was shivering in shock and my legs wobbled beneath me, but I couldn't stop staring at the mangled gore where his genitals once were. I then noticed the fur, clotted, bloody fur and a strand of pink I recognized as the tail of a rat.

The man whimpered in a cracked wheeze of a voice, "It ... won't ... let ... go," and a tear skidded down his stubble cheek. I looked down and realized the rat was alive regardless of the stab wounds it was receiving, gnawing and thrashing and trying to eat its way into the poor man though his crotch. There was nothing I could do to help him. Then the announcement came.

"Ladies and gentlemen, please remain calm. There is a situation we are looking into involving a possible group of aggressive animals. We request everyone to exit at the next staaaaAAAHHH," and the voice blended seamlessly into the most blood curdling scream I'd ever heard, even more haunting and distorted through the subway announcement speakers. I was beyond terrified, my mind reeling with the unfolding nightmare when I saw the movement. Three rats were perched on the other side of the Plexiglas window at the end car a few feet away. They were bobbing their heads and twisting them at odd angles, and I realized they were tearing sizable chunks from the window, trying to get through.

I sprinted to the emergency exit window and yanked at the handle, looking back at the rats that were quickly shredding through the divider between them and me with utter horror. I was finally able to remove the emergency window and hopped out into the narrow space between the subway and wall in the darkened subway tunnel, having twisted my ankle with a sharp pain from the drop. I squeezed by the train hurriedly by the large subway car as quickly as I could in the darkness of the tunnel.

I heard the strange squeals of the rats that I have never heard before, an abnormal noise like high-pitched screaming, echoing from the window behind me as I worked my way to the front of the train down the tracks. I tried not to look up at the next car when the fists pounded on the window, but I did and I saw the rat burrowed into a woman's eye socket, blood and chunks of gore spilling down her face. I struggled to look away as her body lost its ability to function, as her brain had clearly been chewed into, at that twitching movement. I kept sliding past until I was finally ahead of the train and then I ran.

I ran though unknown foul pools of rot and mess, litter, shit, and years of dirt, faster than I ever ran before. I nearly tripped a few times in the darkness on the uneven ground, and I saw the light in the distance grow into the stage of the next platform, filled with people, all with concerned faces. I was blinded by flashing cell phone cameras, gasps, some laughter. I grabbed the arms of the helpful watchers that lifted me up and asked me questions that I was unable to really focus on as a result of shock. I ran out of the platform and I ran for roughly an hour, all the way back to my apartment. I bolted the door and I locked the windows. I tore the fridge out and checked the cracks where my walls and floors met.

I'm not taking the subway anymore, so I may be late to my next interview as well.

MY MOTHER'S DISTURBING PHOTOGRAPHS

I was in the attic going through my mother's old things. She'd just passed away a few days before and I was admiring some photos of her in her youth. I was told to wait a week for my dad to help, but had a free day so I decided to check it out to know what size truck we would need. Apparently, not so large, as there were mainly photos, and her framed, classic portrait work and plenty of still-life. I found some behind that were family photos and took a moment to remember her and look back through time at the lovely woman she'd been in health.

I remembered many of the photos of her wearing cat-eye glasses and gaudy dresses. I loved the odd styles, olive colored counter tops and mod 60s furniture she used to own, those colorful family outings I remember from childhood; my father in his prime, the both of them swirling with love. I saw myself as a baby, sloppy as ever, with a shameless grin that made me laugh. There were also some vacation pics they'd taken when traveling to Egypt, Thailand, and England. I found one cardboard box behind the rest in a corner, however, with photos I'd never before seen and immediately felt that something was wrong.

In the rotting, moldy box tucked away in the attic corner, covered with bird and mouse droppings, there was a leather bound book. I nearly dropped the fuzzy tome when I saw the dent in the cover wasn't a damage mark but was instead shaped like a belly button. The book looked like it was bound in flesh and my skin crawled in revulsion at the discovery, but it must have been a coincidental shape from damage, I thought. I opened it and saw a photo of my mother in a faded pose, standing in a lush jungle, holding a machete and smiling. As I flipped through the next pages I realized the sweet but stern mother I knew was only a fraction of who she'd actually been.

There were photos of her drinking dark liquid from a white, smooth bowl, then photos of severed hands lined up in a row, and pics of my mother wearing some strange head to toe, almost Afghani Pashtun dress, but not quite, with an odd metal crown with three points that rose up from the center. There were also photographs of my mother and a few others in a group wearing similar garments, encircling a pile of what looked like the bodies of children. I was aghast at what I was seeing. I slowly turned the page and saw the awful images I can't bear to think about. The looks on those screaming child faces as they were cut into and dismembered and split struck me profoundly, and soon tears blurred my vision, forcing me to wipe them with my sleeve. I looked at the next page and it confused me. I blinked and tried to understand what I was seeing.

In the next photo, my mother was holding something the size of a swaddled baby, but there were very long things protruding and it visually made no sense. There were multi-articulated jointed limbs protruding from the fabric, like a snow crab's, but with no seams at the joints, just smooth flesh. What they attached to was out of view, but it was almost as if several four-jointed narrow arms or legs were jutting out and about two feet each in length. They tapered to rounded nubs no larger than a pinkie. My mother was facing the camera but looking down and smiling at whatever thing was swathed in those blankets. My neck rippled with a chill and I finally lost the contents of my stomach on the attic floor. I crawled with agony down the shaky stepladder, shuffled my heavy feet into the car, and sat there quivering with fear and disgust, clutching the wheel with white knuckled fists. After 15 minutes of decompressing I finally started the car and drove straight to my father's house.

I hadn't called him beforehand, as I normally do, but this was an emergency and I needed resolution. I drove to his place (they had been separated for over a decade) and was surprised to see an additional black sedan in the driveway. I sent him a text in case he needed me to come back another time to let him know I'd popped by before ringing the bell. After a few minutes I saw his face appear in the front window, staring at me wide-eyed. After a few more minutes I received a text telling me to come in. I approached the front door which opened to my father extending his arms for a hug and I embraced him.

"It's good to see you," my father spoke warmly. "I have a guest over just going over details of Clara's will. You can stick around for this, too, if you'd like. The reading is in a few days, though." I nodded and followed him into the living room, but panic hit me when I saw the man on the couch. He was far older, hair gray and thinning, but clearly one of the figures in those awful photos.

"Mr. Fleishman," the man said while standing, extending a stiff hand in my direction. I nodded and shook the hand reluctantly. On the table lie the printed will and some other documents. I turned to my father and asked, "I'm very parched. Can you help me fix a drink? It's been a rough day." I was trying to signal him with my eyes to go with me but not in any obvious way.

"Sure thing," he replied thankfully, rising to his feet and guiding me with a hand on my shoulder. Once in the kitchen I whispered to my father and explained the book I had found. The massacred children and strange outfits, the thing in the blanket, the drinking of what looked like blood, I mentioned all of it. He looked at me in silence nodding, placing his hand under his chin. "Ahhh," he began with a bit of concern, but less than I'd imagined, "Are you sure this was real? Your mother joined a film crew in Malaysia in the 70's. It was likely that set I'd imagine." A slight relief came over me as I listened to him explain.

I recalled my mother telling me about her old photo work but never film work. My father explained that she felt it undermined her artistic integrity as a photographer so she chose not to bring it up. It actually made sense. Some Zombie Holocaust style foreign gore trash isn't exactly a fine artist's prized resume point. Relief swept over me as I learned that Mr. Fleishman in the other room was her good friend and a credited filmmaker. My father and I pulled up his Wiki of films on my phone and I rested a little easier. Content with the new information, I entered the other room, said my goodbyes after a short exchange of pleasantries, and let my father finish his conversation until the reading of the will in the next few days.

The following day I went to work as usual, glad to have put the nightmarish mess behind me after resolving the mystery. I returned to my mother's house and resumed clearing the attic, hauling the large items first before returning to that box tucked away in the back. The dust was getting to me but I wanted to see more in the new light. I flipped through, and my god, the effects were far beyond anything I'd seen done in the 70s. I smiled, flipping through the jungle sets, replete with smiling cast members, and then saw one that sent a chill up my spine.

It was my mother with the filmmaker's hands on her misshapen stomach above her pelvic area. She was not pregnant, but the next pic showed a horrific looking blade wound exactly where her C-section scar from my birth years later would be. The following photo was blurry; the man was cutting something from her, something half formed, and difficult to identify. It looked like the foetus of an animal I'd never seen. It was slimy, six-armed, and the size of a small octopus, but it appeared to be a mammal. The long joints on its torso resembled the large thing I'd seen her cradling earlier, but was more animal-like. A child was assisting, one that I recognized as one of the slaughtered, mutilated actors before, but they were clearly much younger. I then realized the photos were going backwards rather than in chronological order. He had been cutting her open and placing that thing inside of her.

I flipped through, more and more anxiously through the animals being slaughtered, the blood consumed, the children running up to the plane, then the plane in the air, then finally back in the states to this very house, to a strange crib being placed in a space, to the space being built inside the false wall in this very attic. I looked at my phone's browser history and pulled up the director's filmography once more and read them off one by one, clicking details and discovering they were in fact actual films and that they did exist. I then read something I'd missed before, however, under genre. It was how every single film this man had shot was a documentary with no effects and no actors. One I had glanced over as a "cult classic" read "classic cult doc." I looked up from the area in the photo with a false wall to the actual space I was in and could see that the chamber that was hidden yesterday was now exposed.

In the cloud of black, fuzzy shadow I watched in utter horror as flesh colored appendages maybe six feet long, bent at four joints, extended slowly from the shadows from within to cling outward to the walls beyond. That thing that emerged in half shadow will freeze my blood for the rest of my existence. That drooping, amorphic head with wobbling tendrils of eyes that hung down like digits over the rippled, bony head, the dangling mouth that flared outward in a cone of disgust, flecked with thin, glistening black fangs, the horrific burst of breath it choked out, fading into a bubbling hiss. I scrambled to the hatch as it lunged, falling down the steps in a painful fall, cracking my head. I don't remember the rest as I fled frantically from that attic, into the car, and out the driveway.

I just remember driving, though not to my house. I just drove past when I saw that black car in my driveway. I found a hotel for the night to try and figure out what to do. I only know that I have no desire to know anything more about my family, about my mother, or about whatever thing she hosted as a surrogate. I've been staying away from the windows lately. I just wish my father would pick up his phone, but it's been going straight to voicemail. A black car's been on the block for the last day and a half. My only respite is I can finally get some sleep, as the angry hissing of stray cats through the side window has completely stopped.

BORED OUT OF MY MIND

I ride the train to work daily. It's a slow ride to the city, just about an hour. I try to crank the minutes past by reading news on my tablet and occasionally getting some work done on my laptop, which I also bring on the daily commute. I just miss the peak hour train, which means plenty of room and little crowding, which is one benefit of my current position. Rarely is anything memorable in the morning commute, but today's routine was disrupted less than halfway through. Today I sat facing a man in his sixties two seats ahead, who looked half awake, just staring forward into space. I didn't notice him until 20 minutes into the ride when he slowly spoke the word, "Booooored," to nobody in particular.

You and I both, buddy, I said in my head. I'm no morning person myself, but he looked utterly exhausted, droopy eyes glazed over and distant. He was dressed casually, a navy fleece and neatly combed silver hair, not the sloppy type I'd associate with that kind of outburst. I returned to the article I was reading on my tablet when a few minutes later he uttered, louder and in a drawn out way, "Booored out of my mind." I shot him an irritated look, hopefully getting him to realize nobody cared about his entertainment level. His eyes looked past me, as if he was truly filled with the worst case of ennui I had ever seen. He said it again, "Booored out of my mind," in a dull, low voice, and I rolled my eyes. *This had better not last the entire ride*, I thought.

Don't get me wrong, I often suffered from extreme boredom on this ride that can crawl to a drip of slowly passing seconds. It was just longer than an enjoyable daily commute should be. I looked around the train car and saw a few more passengers, all looking ahead with 10 mile stares of morning fatigue. *This train could seriously use a coffee car*, I thought. I returned to my reading, hoping to escape that feeling myself. I was distracted by a scraping sound, then noticed his arm was outstretched and moving, like he was vandalizing the seat in front of him. He was a bit old to be a graffiti writer, and too clean cut, so something was off. He said it yet again and my face flushed with anger. This was obnoxious and in no way acceptable behavior for an adult, maybe a six-year-old having a temper tantrum. I tried to ignore it and pretended to read, not unable to, and was truly distracted when he spoke again.

"Boooored ou..." I cut him off this time.

"I KNOW! Please keep it to yourself; you're *very* distracting and I'm trying to read. Please." I hate being the rude guy, but this was seriously more annoying than I could bear, and he was being quite rude himself. He kept staring past me with those half-open eyes, and when he continued I got up and walked over to confront him. I was going to say something, anything, not mean or aggressive, just something to raise his awareness, but as I drew closer I saw his shaking hand, pointing.

I realized what he had said differently this time, "... of my, my, leeeggggg," he had droned on in the same, slow and vacant tone. As I got even closer I saw his finger pointing down to the quarter-sized hole in his pants just above the knee. There was fresh blood blooming in his khaki pants, a fleshy raised wound of red pulp and veins oozing from the hole.

I saw the source of the scratching sound now. On the floor was a large, shiny, black beetle, trying to get back on its feet, with far too many legs rapidly clawing at the air than seemed right. It had a sharp, glossy cone of a spiraling shell protruding from its torso like a horrific drill, wide as its entire body and about an inch and a half long. In horror I stepped back, feeling the crunch of one of those ... those things under my heel.

My eyes widened with terror as the man turned his head to the side, revealing a similar, massive hole in the back of his skull, oozing blood, bone fragments and grey matter in chunks down his grey hair like a slow waterfall of gore. I ran down the train car looking at the other nearly lobotomized faces of the other passengers of the car, holes tunneled out of their heads, their arms and their legs. My heart was racing and eyes were wide and tearing, scanning rapidly in fear at the dozens of those horrific insects boring into and out of the seat cushions and body parts of the commuters. I was standing between train cars typing with a drumming heart and with sweat trickling down my temples, horrified. I'll be in the city in about 15 minutes; I just have to make it these endless minutes with my mind spinning with what I can only hope is just fear.

TEETH IN THE SHADOWS

Having finally graduated college, I'd moved to the city and was free to unwind after a very intense final and months of toiling on my thesis. I found a small but sufficient studio apartment downtown with a few bars and coffee shops and it felt like home immediately. I was out my first night enjoying a drink at a bar a few blocks away before eventually sleep tugged at my eyelids. I left the bar a bit after midnight, having lost track of time, and accidentally walked the wrong way to an even more desolate street. Though a bit buzzed, I sobered quickly as I felt the creeping feeling that I was being watched.

I was a bit nervous as I'd heard plenty of stories of people lurking near bars to mug the drunks migrating homeward, and so I swapped my wallet into my front pocket and peeked my head around in search of possible danger. There was a lack of light in the narrow, vacant street, but in an even darker alley merely three meters from where I stood I saw the long teeth barely visible in the shadows under two white orbs. They were far too low, maybe two feet from the ground, wide eyes that were perfect spheres. No eyelids could possibly open that wide. The effect was utterly horrifying.

Below them sat a massive set of teeth reminiscent of the Cheshire Cat's grin, only long and uneven, far too many teeth showing than could be seen under the largest of smiles. Some were chipped, some were bent, and all were slick and white, reflecting what little moonlight penetrated the alley whose shadows concealed the rest of whatever manner of head they were set in. My heart began to beat heavy against my lungs as I tried to figure out what I was looking at.

I told myself to calm down. My inner reasoning told me what I should know, that this was just some mask, sculpture or optical illusion. Maybe it was an alley cat or a stray dog, because monsters don't exist and I was a man of science and reason. Those eyes and teeth were striking a low cord of horror I had not felt in years, however, and I was stuck there staring until the head they rested on cocked diagonally in a rapid motion. And it was then that that unseen thing charged in my direction, sending the message to my brain to run like hell, like a slap in the face which I promptly did.

I sprinted in the opposite direction, looking back, and my dread peaked when I saw the lunging, contorted frame of the figure charging towards me on four thin, deformed limbs that looked human but far more disproportionate. Those wide, intense eyes and bared toothy mouth were fixed on a bald head with a gruesome concave wound where a nose should have been in a ghastly crevice, and it raced towards me as I ran, trying my best to keep distance between us.

My mind was swirling with pure terror as I bolted frantically down the darkened street and then turned into an alley. I froze still, catching my breath and waiting a second, hoping, needing, that thing to lose track of me. It was a mere few seconds when those eyes and teeth rounded into the alley full speed, as if it was a coming straight towards me. I fell backward, muscles rigid and strained with mortal terror, but quickly rose to my feet and continued sprinting down the alley at top speed, short of breath and wondering how long I could continue before I was overtaken. I exited the alley, arced left and looked back to see glimpses of those insane eyes and that smile or grimace of the now clearly lip-less mouth. My brain wanted to rationalize it all but there was no time to do anything but run in abject horror.

The next block was dark and desolate as well, but a lone streetlight at least supplied more light, and yet I still somehow missed the pothole in my panicked fleeing. I tripped to the ground with a painful slap on cold pavement. I saw the ghastly face as the figure rapidly lurched towards me and my heart nearly stopped, as if trying to spare me the fate of that approaching horror. To my shock and surprise, however, the pursuer scurried past me at dead run and it was then that I heard the other set of feet and soon saw the large man with a baseball bat running full speed in my direction. In this new light, things clicked in my head and I grabbed this other man's ankle as he ran past, bringing his large frame down on the concrete with a crack, knocking him unconscious.

I had studied mucocutaneous leishmaniasis (you may not want to look this one up) very briefly in school but it wasn't until the second I was out of immediate danger that I made the connection. It is a rare disease that, left untreated, eats away the mucous membranes of the face and can leave the victim horribly disfigured. Some vile excuse for a man was hunting the poor boy I'd mistaken as chasing me; we were both fleeing in terror. I removed the bat from the brutish man's hands in case he woke as I waited for the police to arrive. I later learned he'd beaten another street kid to death a few weeks prior and it was likely not his first.

I was able to find that poor child, Dymar, about a week later, and he was grateful for helping stop his attacker despite the initial confusion. I began to pay for his medication and restorative surgeries as well. I learned that he'd been born with a joint defect and was abandoned by his mother on the streets, then even more unfortunately, contracting Leish disease. I'm doing my best to help him heal and enter society, and I hope to bring a true smile to his face where he can feel comfortable out of the shadows and away from the streets, and the monsters that roam them at night.

WHY IS HE DANCING?

Sarah asked me this as she looked up with her big brown eyes, freckled face scrunching under her hands as she propped her head up. "One sec, munchkin," I stated without lowering my tablet, just tilting my head around it to see her. I was almost done with the emails and making sure everything on my list was finally finished; it was a hellish week. I was so very close to being done and then we could hop in the car and enjoy a visit to Sarah's grandma, my incredible wife's dear mother. It was only a few hours away but it had been far too long since our last visit due to the busy quarter. I began crunching the numbers, realizing we would be budgeting harder this year.

"Why is he dancing if he's not happy?" Sarah asked me, kicking her legs back and forth in the air as she laid on her stomach. I hated to ignore her, but if I didn't finish my accounting work now we'd have some problems.

"Who, honey?" I asked, not looking up from the numbers, as I couldn't afford to lose my place and restart from the top.

"The man outside. He's dancing but doesn't look happy," she stated calmly. *Was someone outside?* I finished the last line of numbers and finally, with a gap in my tasks, lowered the tablet to look at her. She was the sweetest embodiment of innocence and curiosity and I couldn't have asked for a better daughter.

I smiled warmly and said, "Who's dancing? Are *you* dancing?!" I picked up her feet to lift her upside down and wiggle her back and forth. She burst out laughing but then I heard the dull, ringing slap of skin on glass, startling me. Was somebody *really* outside?

I approached the window and saw a bare leg of somebody rounding the corner of the house until out of view. Something was very off-putting, like there was a strong breeze rippling the pant leg, but I had a mere moment of observation so I couldn't be certain of what. "Go upstairs and make sure you finished packing honey," I advised, then walked to the side of the house where the figure must have then been. After some protest, Sarah agreed and huffed up the stairs.

I headed to the side door and turned on the outside lights illuminating my wife's garden, small, but lovely as usual, but some flowers were clearly trampled. Preparing mentally for a possible conflict, I slipped on my shoes then grabbed the bat from the garage before opening our back door. I heard a kind of stuttering gurgle which sounded like a seizure. I was very familiar with this sound as I'd taken care of my own daughter when she had them before her regimen of the anti-seizure medication Carbamazepine. I ran over to assist, bat still in hand for precaution. What I saw boggled my mind.

There was a man, likely early thirties, doing a spasm-like walk. It was like he was trying to control his muscles but they were trying to do something else entirely. I could only assume it was a seizure at this point and asked, "Sir, are you okay? You may be having a seizure; if you lie down I'll ... my daughter is also...." I stopped mid-sentence as horror flushed over me like a bath of ice water. His pulsating muscles were fluttering off of his bone under the skin. They were rippling in his face, which was making every possible expression in a matter of seconds over and over, absolute terror flashing into the most malicious and wide, toothy grin, scrunched up and wrinkled to stun in a fraction of a second. His biceps and calves pulsated and flexed in impossible ways that looked more painful than anything I could imagine. His eyes bulged out of his head to the point I thought they'd erupt from the sockets.

Sarah's voice peeped from the door behind me. "What is he doing, Daddy?"

"Go inside now, Sarah and dial 911, and tell them a man is having a violent reaction and needs emergency help." I had no idea what this was, but if it was a seizure it was beyond anything I'd seen. I turned to see her face change with fear, which twisted a knife into my heart. I turned back to the man who lurched on jerking legs, shocking me with horror and surprise as he was now directly in front of me.

I could see every bulging, purple vein twitching with the muscles rapidly spasming directly under the thin skin of his face like the death throes of a snake. I gasped loudly as a sweaty, quivering hand grabbed my wrist, and I could feel the rock hard, thrashing muscles in his palm drumming on my hand. It was as if every muscle in his body was an individual creature with the sole desire to leave his skin. I tried to pull back but was unable to, as he was younger, far fitter, and whatever was causing his muscles to backfire made them operate to their full capacity. His hand squeezed and piercing pain flooded my receptors from the pulsating grip on my wrist. I reached in my back pocket with my free hand, grabbing the diazepam pen I keep on me for emergencies, and tried to plunge it into his thigh.

I watched in disbelief as his thigh muscles stretched away entirely from the bone, flaying the thigh wide until it shaped an O-shape under the taut skin. The pen skidded along the porous bone of the femur, now directly beneath with an awful vibratory scraping. Blood spilled out from the shredded gash in crimson droplets and the man's face stretched his mouth into a quivering, baboon-like snarl to reveal the entirety of his large, red gums and gnashing teeth.

He smacked me hard in the face with a flailing, vibrating elbow and the sting was followed by the taste of copper. I spit a hard, white tooth to the grass in a string of saliva and blood. His spasms became more violent now, like a crescendo of bodily rejection. Each muscle ripped with a sickening snapping sound as his contorted body warped with quivering horror, snapping ligaments, and some muscles pierced through flesh and jabbed out through fresh wounds like yams made of meat. His grip loosened slightly and I fell back, losing my wind with a thud. I hurried to my feet and waited for an opening in his rapid, inhuman movements.

I stabbed again, this time puncturing thigh muscle with a ripe jab, adrenaline driving me. I watched the abstract, knotted figure that was once a healthy man drop to his knees and then fall backward to the ground, finally slowing. His form was horrifically altered but stillness eased back into his mostly intact face. He was bleeding through the open gashes of flesh, bone and skin draped thin with large meaty muscle, detached and now relaxed, spilling from the gashes in his blood-shined skin like cow tongues. I ran inside and found Sarah rocking back and forth and crying under the dining room table while clutching her knees. I swept her up and hugged her, tears trailing down my eyes as well.

After the ambulance arrived, I explained everything to the EMTs and to the police officers who looked as terrified as I. After an hour-long light show for the neighbors to gawk at, they left with the man in a stretcher, while I tried hard to shift back into holiday mode to erase the terror we had witnessed. My daughter and I entered the car and hit the road to meet the wife and mother-in-law. My calls to her went unanswered, but was is common where she lives due to only a few cell towers. I waited until Sarah passed out in her seat to turn on the local news on the radio.

There was a series of reports of a possible chemical gas attack causing seizures, but the exact transmission method was unknown. That's what the radio stated anyway, but the developing story was unclear. More importantly, what I saw was no seizure in any Earthly sense. Muscles on their own accord cannot possibility do what I witnessed. We parked and I prayed my wife and her mother were okay, but I dreaded the worst. When I saw the door of the house open and my clearly worried wife emerge, I sprinted to her open arms and cried. We gathered inside for a quaint but lovely holiday meal with our small but resilient family, having a moment of silence for the lives lost and injuries sustained. We listened to the radio as the number of dead grew, eager for information.

I had no appetite but forced myself to eat, at least until I saw the slice of turkey on my fork quivering. The impossibly dead, cooked sliver of succulent turkey was twitching in place in front of my daughter, wife and mother-in-law's horrified eyes. The announcer's voice on the radio was urgently stating a poultry recall, a nationwide contamination of unknown origin. As I write with steady hands, I can for the first time assure you of how utterly thankful we are now that my daughter suffers from seizures, and for her medication we shared together as a family after our Thanksgiving dinner. We are grateful despite the guttural screams from neighboring houses and the steady din of ambulance sirens.

WHEN YOU SEE IT

I've been doing freelance design work for a few months and enjoy the lazy, late mornings and lack of commute, as well as browsing the web to make the day fly by a little faster. I browse Reddit and other sites frequently in search of gems to share with my friends, and often find myself browsing those annoying ad-filled slideshow sites that make you click through mediocre images that don't live up to the clickbait labels. Today I was in the process of exactly this when I stumbled upon a photograph that I will never un-see or forget.

It was a random rabbit hole of links that led me there, some uninspired repost of a "when you see it, you'll shit bricks" image that was almost clever, and then some related links on the side of the page which led to other lists and slideshows. I was lazily clicking through in search of some sort of fulfilment to break the monotony. I clicked through a slideshow of unimpressive links featuring clearly Photoshopped "scary" hidden monsters when a face I recognized popped up on my screen.

It was a picture of me as a child, but there was no shadow of a doubt in my mind. It was a faded film photo of me in striped shorts and I now remember holding my stuffed frog I'd adored as a child. It was me at around the age of five in what looked like a back lawn, but it didn't seem to be my childhood home. It was larger and the woods lingering on the property in the background looked darker, taller, and a bit unsettling to be quite honest. I stared at the photo a bit trying to wrap my head around how this photo existed, and why was it on an internet slideshow, and then my thoughts shifted to what brought me here in the first place. I scoured the photo a little more carefully and saw the dark form at the edge of the woods. I actually had to bring the image into Photoshop to make out the shape, but as I adjusted the contrast and brightness it was there, staring at me from the wood's edge.

People often have a strong opinion of what is terrifying: large fangs, evil eyebrows, clowns with knives. People try repeatedly to create horror films that truly scare but which leave the audience with jump scares and loud sounds after a quiet build-up. I used to believe I knew what scary might look like, but I now know I was wrong. As I stared into the desperate, twisted face of that thing in the photo I only then felt the crippling absolute fear that I now know exists. It had a wide open mouth, screaming in agony, dead eyes and those spread apart teeth on what can't possibly be a human jaw, the hunched form and horrifically warped spine that trailed behind it. I heard a clacking becoming louder and realized then it was my mouse hitting the table. I was shaking violently from an uncontrollable shivering that seized my body.

I left the computer and tried to fix lunch but was unable. I put off my work for the day and tried reverse searching the image on Google with no luck. I looked for a contact email or number on the site and there was none. I clicked "next" in the slideshow to get that image off my screen and my heart stopped. I recognized the next photo: it was my summer camp, me bloody-kneed from an earlier fall in the front row in my muddy shorts and wide grin. Bobby, my new best friend, was next to me giving me rabbit ears on my head with his fingers. And that meme font was there again: "When you see it …" I began to sweat and panic tensed my muscles. I began to search the photo for what hidden nightmare must be and again had no luck, so I decided to bring it into Photoshop and adjust the levels. In the dark patch of shadow behind the cabin I saw that horrific face that caused me to shake uncontrollably, the awful face that is the only thing that will ever truly scare me in this life.

I clicked next, an image of my college dorm upon moving in. I'd taken this photo with a Polaroid camera. The photo was still in a box in my closet, I know this, as I'd just went through it last week. I could see that face outside of the dorm window leering from the wood's edge, just a blur but unmistakable now. My mind was reeling and I felt I was losing balance, losing a tenuous grasp on sanity, and absolute horror climbed my spine in ripples. I ran to the closet and ripped open the box, scattering photos on the wooden floor. I saw the photo, the actual photo and that thing was in it, in the same place, barely identifiable but clearly visible.

I ran to the bathroom overcome with nausea and vomited a painful stream of bile into the sink after a seemingly endless coughing fit. I looked at myself, red eyes bulging with fright and face red and dripping with sweat. I turned on the tap to splash water on my face and attempted to wrap my head around how this was possible, around what that horrible thing in the woods *was*. I was planning my next steps, who to contact and bring into this to help me figure it out, to find the host of this site or what this meant, when I saw it. In the mirror, barely visible behind that translucent shower curtain with those wider than wide white eyes and the horrific black shape below its awful mouth, the thing I can never un-see.

5 NATURAL LIFE HACKS TO BETTER HEALTH

I haven't seen my roommate in a few days and thought nothing much of it until his mother called. She sounded seriously concerned and asked me to put feelers out. Josh is a very active person; he exercises frequently and takes lots of multivitamins and whatnot. He was doing some kind of cleansing thing lately and taking an excessive amount of time in the bathroom. I decided to open his laptop and found a single post titled "5 Natural Life Hacks to Better Health". It reads as follows:

"I found this list of very useful life hacks and wanted to share; it did wonders for me!

1. Use turmeric on body hair: It sounds strange but it works to make your skin fresh and clear follicles and remove unwanted body hair. Using a knife, peel and chop a papaya into small chunks then mash into a pulp. Next, grate a finger-sized piece of raw turmeric root using the smallest grater holes. Mix this together into a paste and rub it into your skin for 20 minutes daily, especially hairy parts of your body. Wash with hot water and shave and repeat this daily. Your body hair growth will eventually slow and you

will be smoother, less hairy, and softer for a longer period of time. This also massages the muscles, breaking down lactic acid and making you tender and looser.

2. Wash using vinegar: Bathing in vinegar softens the skin and makes you look years younger! Do this for a week straight and you'll see the benefits immediately. Simply add ¼ cup of red wine vinegar and ¼ cup of cider vinegar to your bathwater. You can add ¾ cup of olive oil to counterbalance the acidity as well, as this adds a healthy gloss to your hair as well. Additionally, you can add ⅓ cup of soy sauce to the bath for some additional benefits to your follicles. A dollop of honey also gives your skin a healthy shine, so combine these to maximize the benefits!

3. Eat Aloe Vera daily: People carry around a lot of excessive waste, but these high fiber foods will clean out any backup and keep you clean on the inside! Make sure to eat a sliver or two of fresh aloe daily. Chia seeds and flax seeds are also great for this, so make sure you go as much as you can to clear out the tubes and stay healthier and clean. After a week of this, toughen your digestive track with a decent meal by chopping up half a loaf of whole grain bread, onions, carrots and celery and one sprig of parsley. Stir these in with a quarter stick of butter in a pan, a dash of salt and pepper, and sauté for 30 minutes for an excellent healthy meal. Eat for dinner after the last time you "go" before bed to let it work restorative magic overnight.

4. Sleep with fresh air!: Research has proven a flowing breeze is far healthier for the immune system than traditional AC. Invest in a decent fan; a loud one can even keep you asleep through any street noises that can keep you awake. This can prevent sleep apnea and other conditions and help

you achieve a deeper and more regenerative REM cycle. Make sure to leave the window open at least six inches to maximize a natural breeze. If possible, leave the door cracked as well to maintain a circuit of steady airflow. Your immune system will thank you and you might notice the difference in as little as a week!

5. Check out my FREE guide! I made a free guide of stretches and other life hacks and lists and tips! Just PM me with your name and address to mail it (sorry, no P.O. Boxes) a week after following these simple steps, but just make sure not to miss a single day, as sticking to this routine daily will maximize results!"

Aside from that, I can't find anything. His cell phone is here but locked so I can't check the call records. I noticed his window was wide open but that can't be related. We live on the third floor and there have been no ambulances outside lately.

I FOUND A WINDOW TO HELL

Rumors floated around my town about a building for years, a building where within existed a window that opened directly to hell. In the 70s a man killed himself and his family in a brutal murder after claiming to have discovered it a few days earlier. In the 90s a teenage boy who'd attended my school claimed to friends he'd found it, refusing to describe it to anyone. After friends called him a liar and disregarded the claim, Jeremy went missing. He was found in the bottom of an elevator shaft three weeks later on March 24th, 1998, a solemn day for our school. It was always a local legend in our working class neighborhood. But I never thought much of it until I found the note.

I'd been at the library looking for books on finances, trying to somehow stay above water and get more back from taxes that year. I was able to save some money but needed a way to get out of debt. In our library, the tax section is on the opposite side of the same shelf as religion, and as I pulled out a book on deducting I saw through to the other side a bookmark in the spine of a book. I likely would not have noticed it if it wasn't for an unmistakable burgundy hue of dried blood on the paper. I reached through and pulled the book from the other side of the shelf and saw it was a book on death and the afterlife. I pulled the bloody bookmark from the dog-eared pages and read it.

It was a note on an old piece of paper, more accurately an address. Underneath it was a partial smudge of a bloody thumbprint, smaller than mine. I was about to put it back but had a nagging feeling and flipped the book open to see the stamp of the last date it was checked out: March 3rd, 1998, the very day Jeremy went missing. I knew this wasn't a coincidence. I also knew I should have just slid the book back and forgotten about it. I felt the feeling one gets when you drive by a horrific crash but feel the tugging of your head swivel over for a glance without your permission. Curiosity nags at you in a way nothing else can and I knew I had to see what Jeremy had seen. I slipped the blood-stained note in my pocket and unlocked my phone. I entered the address into Maps, clicked on the fastest route, and soon after I hopped on the bus headed in that direction, a mere 15 minutes away.

Nervous anticipation climbed up my spine. I began to sweat profusely and my heart beat rapidly, racked with anxiety, but I just needed to see it. I needed to know that something existed beyond this mundane world, to witness some glimpse, some PROOF of an afterlife, or anything not explained or documented. I was raised Catholic but not since I was very young did I believe in any sort of higher beings or existence beyond death. This was the place, I was sure, that Jeremy had discovered the day he described finding the doorway to hell, and refusing to talk any more about it until he presumably ended his life. I couldn't stop myself from seeing this through.

I jumped off the bus and followed the phone map past buildings in various states of disrepair: corner stores and liquor shops. It wasn't long before I was there, standing in front of an abandoned building with an inviting open door and nobody around, except the occasional homeless person straggling by. I walked in with no difficulty, hesitant but determined. I was hit instantly by the foul odor of water damage and heavy mold.

I put my phone in flashlight mode, grimacing at the filth and litter from countless junkies, looters, vandals and whatnot. Fast food wrappers, caked mud and insulation, spray paint cans and needles were strewn all over; the place was a mess. I went up some rickety stairs to find nothing but rubbish. I searched the walls but found no sign of anything but the windows, cracked and boarded in the dark interior. After 15 minutes I was ready to call it quits when I looked once more at the note in my pocket. The bloody smear under the address was in a peculiar sliver, and after a second long look I realized it was an arrow, facing down. I headed downstairs once more and began kicking at some filth-caked, damp clothing and soiled newspapers before I found it: a hidden basement trap door that cut into the stained carpet.

I carry a Leatherman tool for occasional use, infrequent sure, but always rewarding, and the nailed hatch leading down proved to be one of these occasions. After a few minutes of grunt work, I ripped the rusty nails out and was able to pry the hatch door open. I was jarred by a musty stink of dust and mildew beyond any I'd known, and the decay of long dead rats lingered in the thick, dead air. I crept down the rickety wooden ladder, carefully making sure the rotting rungs wouldn't give way and leave me trapped down there. I noticed it almost immediately, the glow of daylight, and thought it was just a missing brick at first before I realized I was completely underground. Chills ran up my spine anew as I realized what I was seeing was physically impossible.

The wall was a standard concrete grey slab of rust stains aside from a three-inch high, six-inch wide gap, and I approached the daylight glow that illuminated the floating dust of that abandoned basement. It was flickering a bit, and as I walked closer I saw that there were two bulging, wide eyes staring at me from the gap. My heart raced and nearly collapsed in on itself as I heard a horrifying scream burst out from the gap, and I raced up the ladder so fast I nearly had a heart attack. I lay down on the debris, knowing very well how filthy it was, before sitting up and regaining my courage to go down again.

I descended the ladder once more into the filthy depths and stared at the gap. The eyes seemed to be gone and more light danced on the dusty chairs and cluttered plastic buckets in the basement. I approached and saw the most radiant blue glow that drove me closer. I knelt down and peered into the window and saw the most beautiful sky I've ever seen. I saw lush fields of grass and an endless sprawl of landscape. Time didn't seem to exist inside of the place I was looking at. There's no way to describe it, but perhaps just an eternity of bliss and joy, families and children, growing older and younger seemingly at will, singing and hugging and relaxing in the sun. It was infinite and endless, a world of wonder beyond anything I'd seen. It was a window to heaven.

I never saw so many people carefree. I could see great distances through rolling fields of lush green and canopies filled with toucans and tropical birds, animals playing, and fruit giving itself gladly to all the beings within. I saw multiple lifetimes connect with no end, no death, and no suffering. It was just pure, unadulterated happiness and complete peace. It was the most beautiful thing I'd seen and I *needed* to be there.

I felt the edge of the window and pried at it but it wouldn't give even a crumb of dust under my toughest attempts using my steel tool. It was impossible to widen. I stared in awe and wonder, saddened about how I'd found a window to heaven and that it was beyond my reach. I was in a spell that was only broken when I heard giggling children approach from the field I stared so lovingly at, and then my heart sunk as I heard the words spoken from beyond the hole: "Are you ready to see it? Here's the window to hell," followed by their tormenting screams as they stared into our world.

MY FIRST YELP REVIEW

I had been saving for nearly four months with my meager income before I could afford to eat here. As much as I wished I could shower my wife with luxurious dinners and our own apartment, I could not. When I finally booked the reservation, the rush was instant and I couldn't wait to surprise her. She tried at first to convince me to save it for our bills or for getting us out of debt, but when I explained that I needed to do this to show her she's worth more than anything and anyone on this Earth, she finally agreed.

I'd read about this place in a few blogs that I check out on my lunch break and it sounded absolutely amazing. It had a renowned French chef with two Michelin stars, celebrities on the waitlist, and was the real deal. I called an Uber since our car is a jalopy of duct tape proportions and I wanted us to arrive in style. The place was decadent, absolutely stunning, and we approached the golden awning and valet area with glazed eyes. I tried my best to act casual as if I was used to this level of luxury, but I felt like a giddy child on Christmas morning. I know my wife felt self-conscious with her knockoff earrings and handbag, but I showered her with sweet nothings and her courage outshined her trepidation. The doorman was the first thing that woke me from the spell.

He simply moved in front of the door rather than open it and stared at me down the end of his nose. It was subtle but unmistakable. He smelled us out and knew we didn't belong; it hurt my heart and my spirits sank. It felt like an eternity but he finally spoke, "Do you have reservations?"

I instantly yelled, "*Yes*, we *do*!" in his smug, rodent face. He shied away, defeated by the revelation, and we stepped into the massive establishment. It was lavish. I'd never been any place so exquisite. Swarovski chandeliers, medieval tapestries, and the most beautiful patrons peeled from Vogue magazine lined the walls. Many familiar celebrity faces laughed and drank champagne, twirled pasta and shared stories. It was a dream until we met the hostess.

She was beyond a supermodel, perhaps 21 but likely younger, and she was wearing a dress that cost my annual salary. She smiled wide-eyed and looked me up and down as if unable to take me seriously. I was wearing a suit, a hand-me-down from my father before his funeral. It was old but I looked fine I'd thought, but she made me feel like absolute garbage with her stare. I tried my best to suppress my feelings and explained we had a reservation. She looked at the list, trying not to smirk and eventually spotted us, exclaiming, "Ahhh, yes, here you are," giving me one more look that seemed to shout, "Seriously?" before slamming the book on the podium.

She led us in past a few A-list celebs I won't name: beautiful people, sports stars, supermodels, and some people we'd just watched in a few films that week. I held my wife's hand proudly, trying to feed her the confidence she deserved despite being overwhelmed myself. The hostess led us back and past them, further into the cavernous restaurant. The food looked and smelled amazing and my excitement built despite the cold greeting. We were led further in, into another room that was a little less impressive and then past that even to a carpeted stairway. We followed the hostess down to a less crowded and clearly less decorated room. I almost said something but just followed as she led us out of that room into a smaller, dingier area with exhausted people slumped at the table. After a few glances I realized these were cooks on break. They were slouched, and some were smoking, napping or drinking beer. It wasn't until we left that room that I had to say something.

We left the basement room into a grimy industrial hallway, grease stains and a wet concrete floor. There were mops, broken dishes and flickering fluorescent lights. There were filthy stains on the wall. It was a mess. Finally, I squeezed my wife's hand and demanded an answer with, "Where are you taking us?" She didn't turn around, merely walked down the hallway, mocking us with her perfect model ass, swaying with luscious moxie. I wanted to take my wife out of there but I'd saved for months and I was determined to treat my wife to a gourmet dinner she so richly deserved. I followed reluctantly as we entered a horrible room.

Through the metal door we entered a dark area that felt cold and smelled horrible. The odor of death instantly accosted our senses, and I pulled my wife's hand to leave but the metal door had locked behind us. It was then the creeping dread rose and the blood drained from my face. There were flies, hundreds of them, buzzing around, picking at the filth on those tables. It was dark but I already knew it was clearly butchered human corpses. My mind began to swirl and I couldn't peel my eyes away. There were pigs and human bodies sewn together in the most disgusting horrors, genitals and eyeballs, intestines and peeled faces, and there was nothing I'd seen in my life to prepare me for the vulgar shock of those mutilated corpses in that room. My wife was shaking and I hugged her close. "Run," I admonished, tugging her hand and leading her straight to the duct.

People look at me and merely see a struggling custodial worker cleaning the floor with a mop. My salary pays far less than I need to thrive, likely far less than yours, but I have a set of skills that are unmistakable and occasionally priceless. I've cleaned the public high school's vents dozens of times, and I am well aware of how to navigate them. Another thing I learned is to keep tools on me at all times, and in that hand-me-down suit pocket was my stainless steel precision screwdriver set. I reacted instantly. It was open by the time a fat, naked man with a machete sauntered into the room, coated with what only could be blood and fecal matter. I helped my wife in first and we sped through faster than you'd think possible, fleeing for our lives.

We bent around a few corners in that vent and soon reached a grate I helped my wife open. We slipped out from the building into an alley with dumpsters and trash bags stacked over my head. My wife was clearly in shock so I hugged her and kissed her, just happy to be away from the terror we'd witnessed. I called a taxi and we rode in silence, reeling from the nightmare we'd escaped. It wasn't until we pulled over and exited next to the quaint diner we frequent regularly that I finally saw her beautiful smile.

[REDACTED] LOBSTER DOES NOT SELL SCORPION MEAT

I received an odd letter today to the previous tenant I wanted to share. I never open previous tenants' mail, but this was from a legal team and looked to be important. I moved in last week, purchasing the Californian duplex directly from the owner, who seemed in a rush to move with his wife and daughter. It read as follows:

7/21/████

Dear ████████ ██████

    The settlement offer contained in this letter is made pursuant to sections 1152 and 1154 of the California Evidence Code. As such, it cannot be used to prove or disprove liability, or lack thereof, of any party of the entitled action, nor can it be used to prove the invalidity of the claim, or any part of it.

    I am authorized to offer the amount of $████████.██ as full and complete compensation for all damages suffered by, and attorney fees and court costs by, your client, ███████ ██████ in the above-entitled action. As per your request, we have included the events that transpired according to your client, which is not an admittance of liability. Our client implored us to iterate the statement "████ Lobster does NOT sell scorpion meat."

According to your client, he and his family frequented our ████ ██████ California location on the evening of 7/2/17. After what was described as a standard family dinner, we are aware your client's son, █████ █████ excused himself to use the restroom. After a 15-minute period of absence, your client claims he left the table to search the restroom and could not find █████ █████, and thus grew concerned. Though the door to the kitchen is locked at this particular establishment, your client claims he waited until it was opened by a busser and slipped in, in search of █████ █████. He further claims he saw an additional back kitchen that looked out of order from a standard kitchen and (illegally) trespassed into said area.

Once inside, your client claims to have seen large tanks with mammoth sized insects, fictitious "aquatic Brazilian centipedes," a fabrication of deceased author ██████ ████████, as well as "horrifically large scorpions," supposedly chewing through the meat of live "rabbits, groundhogs and what looked like stray cats" after stinging them with "large snake-sized stingers." Your client then claims he saw a "harvesting station" in which these large insects were hung on black chains, flash boiled, and then "chopped with cleavers and decorated to mimic lobster tails" by a team of fully suited individuals with protective gear .

Your client then stated he noticed a trail of fresh blood winding back into another side room where he discovered a shoe of a very popular and common brand that he claims was his son's exact sneaker, though no evidence of this remains as your client claims to have fled the area in horror to his wife and daughter. He claims to have seen a "massive scorpion flailing over a pile of mangled flesh and gore, flicking its tail at him," causing him to flee as it struck at him, then causing a scene by screaming outrage on a tabletop, a trespass that led to the loss of thousands of dollars as people fled the restaurant afterward with unpaid tabs.

Your client then claims he returned to the back of the establishment after rounding up a few "large, angry customers" demanding an explanation and the location of his son, but the kitchen doors were locked and impenetrable despite the clear damage (costing the amount of $██████) your client and said men inflicted to said doors. When the police eventually arrived there was an unfortunate fire in the kitchen and the establishment had to be vacated until the ████ ███████ fire department arrived. Your client then became more hostile, claiming the unfortunate incident (which claimed ██ of the location's staff's lives) was a cover-up in an attempt to destroy evidence.

It is my sincere intention to settle this matter amicably, which is why our client is making this settlement offer. We will not sue due for defamation despite your client's slanderous blog, which has made it onto a local news program and has been hurting our client's sales since the rebuild of our client's ████ ██████ location. Additionally, we have a $████ gift certificate to the renovated location and we sincerely encourage your client to frequent the improved establishment. Our client is hand delivering this gift certificate this afternoon and they should be there shortly as a courtesy.

Hopefully this matter should be fully resolved and you and yours will enjoy your free lobster dinner.

Very truly yours,
████ ██████

I thought it must be a very intricate joke at first, though I was surprised by the seal and professional delivery, but I'm feeling a bit uneasy since reading it. A large black box truck has been parked in my driveway for half an hour, and they just reversed to point that the cargo doors are directly in front of my garage.

MY OFFICE BUILDING IS CRACKING

I am terrified of earthquakes and have been my entire life, a condition known as Seismophobia. I grew up in Santa Monica and experienced a horrifying quake as a small child that left my pet fish dead and shattered glass, cutting me up badly enough to require 21 stitches. Once I had the opportunity to head to college on a partial scholarship in New York City, I eagerly jumped on the airplane and figured the horrific rumbling of the Earth cracking beneath me would be a fading memory. My confidence slowly grew to support this as I moved into a recently renovated Brooklyn apartment, and the only rumbling I knew in my new life was the subway ride to midtown and my stomach just before lunch. This changed last week as I stayed late after work to finish editing a few articles I'd been assigned.

I sat at my desk in the dimming daylight, scanning a political piece for errors with a half-eaten turkey club in my hand. My boss had just waved goodnight and told me to shut the lights off and lockup on my way out, a routine I was used to by now, over half a year into the job. I was even okay with working on the 12th floor by now, as there were no earthquakes in NYC as far as I knew since 1992, a fact I treasured dearly. As I wrapped the article up, however, I heard the dreaded sound that perked my ears and raised every last hair on my skin: an unmistakable cracking sound. I finished my edits, panicked and sweaty, trying my best to ignore the endless barrage of images my mind created of me crushed like a fly beneath tons of cement and steel, squeezed of all fluids and organs. By the time I made it home, I was so freaked out it took me until 4 a.m. to fall asleep.

I nearly called out the next day but forced myself to go in, as I needed the job, and any seismic activity would likely not strike again. I asked my coworkers if they felt an earthquake the night before and they assured me they hadn't. After asking the boss, however, he informed me the building had undergone renovations almost a year ago and that some construction workers occasionally worked on it after standard business hours. He assured me it was likely just that. Partially pacified by his response, I carried on with my duties that week and began feeling a bit less concerned. I'd looked it up online and there was no report of any minor quake in the area. It was Friday when a second event sent me spinning into a fit of terror.

Again staying late, I was finishing the final edits on a piece when I heard the cracking sound that froze me to the core. We had a large pillar in the room and I stared in absolute horror as I saw a large crack split down it before my eyes. I ran to the elevator, leaving my work unfinished and the door unlocked that evening. I called the boss once outside and he seemed concerned but understanding of the situation. I tried my best to relax that weekend but was unable to get images of falling to my death and being crushed by glass and steel out of my head. When I returned to the office on Monday I was a ball of nerves and unintentionally snapped at my coworkers who'd asked how my weekend had been. "FINE, *okay?*" was all I could express in a voice that scared even me.

That particular day I stared at the pillar every few seconds, just waiting for it to fully collapse and for the ceiling to implode inward, devouring us all and folding our bones into splintered, compact origami in the dust. As my dreaded fears crawled to life before my very eyes, I heard another loud crack and stared, jaw agape in a horrible grimace, as a massive block of plaster split off the pillar and crumbled to pieces on the ground. It was cinematic, cracking off slowly as if in low gravity. I hadn't truly felt the full impact of post-traumatic stress before, but this is what was happening to me.

I collapsed off the wheeled, adjustable office chair and spilled onto the floor in slow motion, staring at the pillar and the writhing movement from within. There was something alive in the pillar, something squirming, chalky white and smooth, almost familiar. I passed out and it wasn't until I came to with an oxygen mask covering my mouth from the EMTs that I could finally understand what I'd been looking at.

Through the months at the office there were occasionally union workers on megaphones protesting the building owner for their cheap and unethical construction methods. They never hired union, never paid fairly, and apparently had a massive list of violations and an incredible amount of negligence. It turns out a worker had somehow fallen into the plaster mold when the decorative pillar was poured and nobody had seen this, assuming he'd just quit due to the brutal, unsafe work and horrible pay. He should've died after mere minutes, but a series of tragic events prevented his death as some extra debris and piping ended up creating an airway for the poor man, and a steady leak from the gap had supplied a steady stream of drinking water that carried down bread crumbs from the roof where a custodian fed pigeons daily. The man had survived, buried in this god-awful tomb for almost an entire year, frozen in painful darkness.

I'll spare you the horrific details of the atrophied limbs, the waste that impacted until it ravaged his organs, and of what happened to his fragile, peeling skin. The man was brain damaged and died soon after his removal. My boss offered to pay for therapy for our entire team after the event, which I might have taken advantage of. My fear of earthquakes has subsided. Well, not exactly subsided per se. I think it has simply been overtaken by my new staggering fear: the endless nightmare of getting entombed alive, a fear that sent me screaming out the door and emailing a resignation letter yesterday after the elevator dropped a foot and froze in place, leaving me paralyzed in a fit of terror in the darkness for nearly half an hour.

EEEEE

I'm a fairly secure person with little fear, perhaps to my disadvantage. I have no issues walking through what my friends refer to as "bad neighborhoods". I always meet kind and welcoming people wherever I go, and perhaps it's a reflection of my own respect for others, but I have had few unwelcoming experiences with strangers. I have a brother named Roger with Down Syndrome, my best friend who I love dearly and who's active in a few special needs groups. He's become great, long-time friends with a few people from these groups since he was a tot. His best friend Alan lives in one of these "bad neighborhoods" and I have to walk under a rather poorly lit underpass to get from the parking garage to his tenement. When I headed over to pick him up today things took a disturbing turn.

I was running late and after scalding myself with spilled coffee, I tried to dress quickly and dash out the door, nearly forgetting the baseball. Alan and Roger basically share it, a baseball they both caught in a show of brilliant teamwork on one of our outings at the stadium. They have me deliver it back and forth each time we meet as a sort of peacekeeping ritual, and I learned my lesson to not let them down by forgetting it. I stared at the clock in dread; I was 15 minutes behind schedule and would need to skip breakfast due to having overslept.

I'd somehow managed to kick my alarm clock out of the socket, leaving it unplugged during the night, and the last thing I wanted was Alan waiting outside near that busy street for me. I repeatedly suggested to his mother that he should wait *inside* until I called her, but she was less than attentive to his needs, to put it lightly. I entered the minivan and gunned it, headed towards Alan's neighborhood. I was speeding to make up for lost time. When my phone rang over the radio speaker, loudly and unexpectedly, I swerved from the sudden sound, nearly clipping a tractor trailer. I'd pulled over in a state of panic to settle my nerves. I had answered and immediately began apologizing to Alan's mother for being late before heading back onto the road, frazzled by the day's rough start.

I finally arrived, parking the minivan in the 4th story of the garage and exited the vehicle noticing the chill from a strong breeze. Fast food bags and other various litter swirled in slow dust devils and a candy bar wrapper slapped my face, covering my eyes in a gust of wind. I cursed and removed it, agitated by my seemingly endless bad luck this particular day. I hadn't realized just how bad it was until I noticed a figure standing in the corner of the dark garage.

He was barefoot, facing the corner away from me, with slumped shoulders and was just bobbing his head up and down in the dark shadow of the corner's crease. I called out to ask if he was okay but he didn't respond. I began to feel truly creeped out by his peculiar behavior. There was something that told me to get out of there, but I was concerned that this person might need help or have a condition needing treatment, so I approached, asking again if he was okay and if he was lost. When I approached with an extended hand to place on the figure's shoulder, he turned to me with a hideous face I can't forget.

The face looked as if the skull had been removed and replaced with that of a large deer or pig, elongated and poorly fitting, jutting outward in a shocking angle, wearing it thin and translucent with windy veins beneath and blotches of bruising. There were long black holes devoid of eyeballs spilling out what looked like dead or dying flies, and a large gummy maw with twisted yellow teeth, resting in the large, horrendous smile of a mouth that screamed, "EEEEEE!" in a horrible high-pitched screech as the figure spun and began charging at me full speed.

I have been around my share of hostile individuals, some having temper tantrums, others with the inability to understand a situation properly, and still others just drunk and attempting to act macho at a bar. I almost always know the best course of action to respond to with these individuals, usually talking, sometimes a hug, or with regard to the latter an occasional fist. In this instance there was only one single thing that was an option as terror rippled up my spine, and that was to *run*. I bolted straight to the stairwell as that screeching, "EEEEEE!" echoed on the dirty cement walls in that vacant garage behind me, chilling me to the core beyond any sound I have ever heard on this Earth. I smashed into the concrete wall rounding the stairwell going down but kept my footing, sprinting down flight after flight past the empty cars, the filth and the debris. I was gaining ground from the horrific screaming pursuer but knew the exit out was on the bottom floor past that tunnel, past that horrid underpass below the interstate that was just a bit too dark and much too long.

As I finally rounded the bottom stairs I faced that dim, yellow tunnel, the stench of urine and other murk assaulting my senses under those flickering, yellow fluorescent lights. It was longer, at least twice as long as it had been in memory since my last visit, and I stared down the eerie passageway. I cocked my head upwards to listen to the brooding shadow of the stairwell behind me and heard nothing. I must have outran whatever that ... thing had been, at least for now. I just needed to make it outside and call the authorities after I picked up Alan.

I briskly walked down the cold, noxious-smelling underground corridor, bewildered at the length of it, my fists balled in apprehension. My steps echoed and I heard an additional shuffled echo synched up with them but clearly separate from my own. I turned, heart pounding in my chest, and saw that horrible face that screeched, "EEEEEE!" in response while speeding towards me, its dirty bare feet slapping the stained concrete and hurdling towards me at a full sprint. I ran for my life and was gaining distance in that elongated hallway towards the hazy bright light of the now visible exit. I stopped myself short and spun around, running back into the depths of that nightmarish underpass towards the horrific screaming thing in the hall.

If you knew Alan, you'd know how heartbroken he'd have been had I not brought it. If I walked up to him empty-handed, he'd be crushed. I'd observed his face the last time that happened and I swore to him I wouldn't forget it again. The look on his face was the one thing that propelled me as I faced my terrifying pursuer, running towards that nightmarish, screaming horror. I squeezed my eyes shut, ducked low, and passed it as I sprinted back to the dark stairwell, exhausted as my blood pumped hot in my veins as I climbed those four flights of stairs. I ran all the way back to the van as that screeching, "EEEEEE!" resonated in my ears trailing behind me. I saw the baseball on the back seat and hurriedly flung the door open, hopping in the front seat to reach it.

My eyes finally opened as my minivan skidded with the awful screeching, "EEEEEE!" of road-grinding tires as I spun out from the brutal collision, stopping against the guardrail of the highway with a thud. The tractor trailer had crumpled the front of the van and had left my leg pinned. I knew it was crushed and the pain would come later on. My head was bleeding heavily, but I was alive, once again conscious and alive. A man leaned into my shattered window and told me an ambulance was on its way and to remain still, but I refused to obey. I found my phone and made the call to Alan's mom, telling her I'd been in a car accident and to make sure Alan was away from the street and indoors, and to tell him that I had his baseball for him as soon as I saw him.

That wasn't for another two weeks, after I was finally released from the hospital with a heavy cast and a bandaged head when I was able to hand back Roger and Alan's shared baseball to them, the baseball that brought me back away from that light at the end of that underpass, returning me to my life.

I THINK MY BOSS IS GOING INSANE

Currently I live in NYC, and have been for a few years now, jumping from startup to startup that tried their best but just didn't take off how they needed to. I'd been unemployed for a few months when I found a new job via a recruiter. It seemed like a decent place and a great location, and frankly living on Ramen and scouring the web for small freelance gigs wasn't cutting it. I went in for the interview to meet the team and to present them with my experience.

Upon arriving, I met my employer, who was a much older man in his 70s, well-dressed but clearly a bit awkward socially. He shook my hand firmly and stared into my eyes for a second or two, which felt a bit odd, and then he sat down. "Show me what you've got!" he said, and I went through my portfolio, detailing each project and process, making sure to highlight my skills. After about 10 minutes he gestured dismissively and I was sure I didn't get the job. He thanked me for my time and said he'd be in touch. I was utterly surprised when he sent a wordy, handwritten letter asking me to start the following Monday.

Returning to the office, everything seemed to be standard. He seated me in a smaller room and gave me a set of sites to research and some lists to compile and outline my strategy, totally normal stuff.

He explained he was busy setting up conferences so I'd be writing some emails as well, converting handwritten notes to emails. This was not at all related to my skillset, but I'm a fast typist so this was more of a relaxing meditative exercise than work, so I honestly didn't mind. His handwriting was a bit hard to read, so I had to stare for a bit to make out some of the words.

So for the first few weeks the letters I'd converted to email were totally normal: "Dear Mr. Stanton: We have an excellent business opportunity and are seeking funding..." It was content about seeking to partner, promises of stock guaranteed to jump, etc., nothing unfamiliar with my line of work. Occasionally an odd word was placed here or there, so assuming I didn't read them properly, I made a list of some I had noticed. These were sentences like: "Alas, Mrs Fielding, I wanted to speak to you", or, "Sentiments Danny Fischer! I am writing in regards..." etc. etc.

Eventually I spoke to my employer who just said to leave them, as he wanted his own "character" in the message, so I shrugged and agreed. His writing, however, seemed to get worse, and I had trouble straining my eyes to try and read the letters. Additionally, his wording seemed to become more peculiar, unprofessional to the point that I had to let him know it would affect potential sales. Sentences like, "Pleased be, our service is remarkable", and "Otherwise grateful to speak", were followed by his signature. I approached him and he seemed furious at my questioning him, wrinkling his lip into an angry sneer, and then relaxing into a wide-eyed stare, then a smile and strange laugh that chilled me. "I'm not really mad. Leave them be and just do your job. We've a busy month!" he spouted chipper, and then shooed me out of his office.

A week or two passed when I began having some serious eyestrain from the deteriorating handwriting. My boss remained hunched in his office manically scrawling handwritten notes and scouring on old yellow pages. Translating those seemed to be my *only* current role. Furthermore, they made less and less sense each time, as he was not even asking for funding anymore. Sentences had degenerated and paragraphs were shortened into insane ramblings. Occasionally when I'd pass his office, I'd see him hunched over, leering at me with strange, wide eyes and heavy breathing.

Nearly every letter was becoming more cryptic and nonsensical. My eyes had been killing me and blurring up a bit as well. I noticed serious carpel tunnel from so much typing, not what I imagined when signing up for this gig either.

Dementia seemed like a probable cause. I'd rather have you see for yourself. Here is one of the last letters I had to send via email:

"Pleasure to meet you, Anna.

Only my great opportunity could be this driving, and of all the days! We've had quite the year, in finance and international events, yes? So many twists and turns!! It's like a reality television show, I'd say!?! Do you watch the news, Anna? If so, you must know how much effort is put into a production. All the tiny players acting out like cogs in a machine. May this find you well!

Xavier Hertsfield, pleasure to meet you!

Oh, I have an opportunity at hand, nearly got carried away!

Nearly forgot to mention.

You can email my employer for details:

Omar Urlech, urlech.omar@(myemailaddress, etc. etc.).com"

Nearly every letter has been lacking in any description and I know they are not related, but my life seems to be getting worse every day as my job makes less and less sense. My knuckles have swollen up from the endless typing and ache horribly, blisters rise near my fingertips. My vision has blurred and I've been prescribed glasses—10 in my left eye—12 in my other. I've had perfect vision my entire life until now.

Other than that, my girlfriend left me after calling me disgusting and saying she couldn't stand me anymore, and I just found out my landlord refused to renew due to some horrible odor he insists is coming from my apartment. I take the trash out regularly and have had nothing to do with it but he refuses to listen. I can't quit this job as it is the only thing currently keeping me afloat. I knew they couldn't be connected but I stayed late one day after my boss left and noticed the very strange books on his office shelf.

Witchcraft, ancient lore, rituals. There were mildewed, dust-covered books on subliminal messaging, hypnosis, word puzzles and thesauruses. It was a strange find. I noticed many highlighted words in a few of these tomes, especially the one that seems in connection with my boss's letters, the broken paragraph structure of focusing on the first letter within. Things are just too horrible now and I'll do whatever I must at this point. I'm truly sorry ...

I'VE WITNESSED A DISTURBING BREAK-IN

I loved my apartment, and living alone in my sun-drenched pad, made use of the gym and the laundry facilities on every floor. I had some great times here with wonderful friends that turned the biting cold of winter into a pleasant nibble. I was safe, solo, and single, feeling the woes of the last four struggled years fizzle away in a warm cup of hot cocoa in front of my new 50" TV. I loved the view as well, and I went to the window to enjoy the skyline, a magnificent panorama of Manhattan beaming speckled stars of color across the dusk sky. The view was obstructed by one neighboring apartment building, nothing complaint-worthy, however.

The building that stood less than ten meters from mine was even more lavish, beyond my price range, and it definitely showed. It had a lovely exposed brick interior on the back wall with a large floor to ceiling window, and I could see through the empty apartment and vast window to the window of the building past it. I notice some movement and my gaze drifted to it, noticing a figure through the window across the street from mine, and knew right away something was very wrong. A figure scuttled clumsily down the black metal fire escape to enter the view of the visible building that sent shivers down my spine.

As an avid birdwatcher, I own a few sets of binoculars but I'm no Peeping Tom. I mind my own business and never pry, but this was a situation straight out of *Rear Window*, so I fetched my Nikon Prostaff and got a better look at the unfurling scene. I immediately knew when I saw the face zoomed in what I was witnessing. It was hanging slack and the man had apparently suffered from a stroke, and he was also bleeding heavily from his nose and mouth. Blood streaked his drooping, broken skin as if melting with a ghastly weight. I knew instantly he must have threatening injuries and I raised my phone and entered 911, ready to dial. The phone in my hand lowered to my side, however, as I watched him hastily remove a screwdriver from his worn, black leather coat.

The look on that face, whenever in view and not facing the window of that apartment, was one of crawling horror, jaw agape and bloodied to the point that I shuddered at imagining who, or what, he was fleeing from. I watched in both awe and horror as that window across the way slid up and the large man stepped slowly over the open sill and into the apartment. There was a handprint of thick blood on the window. This man would likely die of blood loss and whoever he'd escaped from was likely in the stairwell and at that apartment door. I picked up the cell and mapped in the address of the building as best as I could guess. My phone buzzed, jarring me with a scare, and I dropped it to the floor.

My neighbor Jerry and I, I remembered, were supposed to hit up the park that day, but that would have to wait. I ignored the call and dialed 911, anxiously awaiting the operator's answer. Eventually I was able to speak to an operator and explain what I had seen and the location of the building in relation to mine. She asked for additional details and I resorted to hopping on Google Maps and realized the building on the other side of the obstructing apartment wasn't on Maps. Instead, it showed there was a freeway there which was impossible. And then I heard it: a shuffling sound that was coming from the next room. I spun my head in horror to see my neighbor, Jerry, face slack and dangling, smeared with trails of blood as he walked into view. Immediate terror iced my veins, and at this distance Jerry's face was clearly detached from the head of the man's own it was placed over. In a panic I picked up my laptop and sprinted to the bathroom, slamming the door shut moments before the straight razor lashed towards me, slicing my finger to the bone in the sliver of the closing door and frame.

As I sit here bleeding, hand wrapped in a blood-soaked towel under my armpit, I'm wondering how long the police will take to arrive. I called them a few minutes ago and just have to wait and see who will get to me first. I only wish I'd called them sooner or had known then what I do now. That window in the next apartment was actually a full length mirror and I had been watching my own apartment being broken into by the killer of my upstairs neighbor, Jerry, now wearing his face as a mask.

PEOPLE, PLACES, THINGS

My memory is exceptional. I can remember the year, the month and the day of my first lost tooth, my parent's divorce, our pet's death, and my first bill. My friends called me a weirdo but my condition has uses as well. I never forget their birthdays, their anniversaries of lost loved ones, and I am extra sensitive to them on those particular days. I know every block of this city like the back of my hand, which has three scars from three separate childhood accidents, of which I also know the exact dates of, and which is shaking a bit now making it difficult to type. I'm not autistic as far as I know, but our family physician on April 14th, 1992 explained I likely had Hyperthymesia, an abnormally excellent memory. I'm also a very careful person. I walk faster and with more precision than most bumbling, cellphone abusing people, and am attentive enough to slip past these slower people with no difficulty. Yesterday, however, my precise sliding past a slow, elderly woman into the subway blocking the door didn't go as planned.

The door was closing and the woman had just entered, obstructing most of the entrance. I couldn't afford to be late so I slipped by, but at that moment, she turned, causing me to knock the previously unseen book she was holding out of her hands and onto the subway car floor. I reached down to pick it up, some sort of notebook or sketchpad, but was intercepted by another man who returned her book before I had a chance. I apologized but received an angry glare that wrinkled across her sickly, pale face. She slowly hobbled towards a seat and then sat before staring at me with wide, hateful eyes and a ghastly frown that shook me to the core.

She must've been in her 80s, her grey hair thinning and matted under a faded red headscarf snaking down her wrinkled, spotted face in sweaty tendrils. Her red lipstick was a few shades too dark on her slightly agape mouth, a blood red wound framed in a tight knit of wrinkles and moles, oozing a stream of drool down her cheek. Her wide, staring eyes were horrific, porcelain orbs, yellowed and bloodshot, pupils faded with cataracts but still piercing into me like needles from her seat. I forced myself to look away, aiming my eyes at ads and at my feet but unable to not see that intense stare.

After a few minutes I noticed the woman's hands opening a book, pages obscured by the angle, and she procured scissors from her brown bag and began to cut pages with them. Her intense stare was still fixed on me so I didn't look directly, but I could tell she was cutting vigorously, chopping at unseen pages while darting those horrible eyes at me. I desperately wanted to leave, so I decided to get off at a station before mine, as 10 blocks of walking was better than this tortuous woman's hateful glaring. I mouthed a genuine "I'm sorry!" to her right before walking out the sliding door and I was chilled to hear a loud, hysterical, rage-filled laughing explode from her crinkled mouth as I exited the train.

I rushed up the stairs and began walking towards my workplace, and I passed the cafe and news stand and stopped dead in my tracks. My office building was on the next block ahead of me. The entire block was exactly as it should be, but it was far closer to the subway than possible. It was as if seven entire city blocks were simply gone. I stared dumbfounded and looked around to see if others were confused and nobody seemed to notice a thing. I wiped my eyes and walked to the street sign and it read 34th. My office had always been on 40th. I was bewildered and stunned so I asked a stranger where 34th street was, praying my eyes were playing tricks on me, but he just pointed up at the street sign and said, "Right here."

I was always more observant of people maneuvering in and out of my path, and rarely got off at this stop, so I couldn't state every single store and building that was missing but I knew many were gone. I was already late so I briskly picked up my pace. The day was busy but I had time to Google Map the area. It was seamlessly compacted into a smaller version of Manhattan. Even Brooklyn was shorter. I refreshed and searched for addresses I knew by heart in the area (I know many) and they were all missing completely or changed to match the alteration.

At the end of the day I was freaked out thoroughly as I stood by the elevator. This was impossible; it couldn't be happening. The spell of terror was snapped by a voice, "You getting on, buddy?"

I spun and entered the elevator, reeling now just how much sweat was pouring down my face. I pulled out my phone to text Alyssa, my girlfriend, but in my minimized message list her name was gone. I opened contacts, opened emails, opened my photo gallery, terrified and likely looking like a maniac and found nothing, not a single trace of her. I was visibly shivering now, my phone shaking in my quivering hands. "I'm going insane," I thought, and I walked out the elevator to the street, the subway stop now in view from my current office location. I texted my friend that I needed to meet and that it was an emergency. He agreed and so I walked down a few blocks to a bar and ordered a beer to calm my nerves.

Sean came in, smile on his face, and asked what was up as he slid into the seat across from me. He ordered a beer and I asked him if he had fun hanging with Alyssa and I over the weekend, as we'd eaten at a great new seafood place on Sunday. He stared, confused at me like I was mad. "Who's Alyssa?" he asked. "You met up with Beth and me for some food." My heart shattered in my chest and I felt tears welling up in my eyes. I know you've all felt loss before but this was the absolute worst kind imaginable, as there was no shred of her ever having existed and my memories were now 100% false. I explained the story of the woman on the train and the day's events and he looked at me with a sad, wary gaze and said he really thought I needed help.

I tried to explain, "I know how insane I must sound," but I could see the look in his eyes, the look one gets when they are far beyond help and clearly unable to be related to. Sean left a $10 bill on the table, excused himself and left, expressing concern and wishing me well. I picked up my phone after a few minutes to text an apology only to see his number wasn't there anymore. I asked the waitress about the man who she'd served and just received a confused look.

I searched through my contacts and realized only a fifth of them remained. My parents were in there but my brother who lived in Brooklyn was gone and most of my friends were also gone. I got on the subway and saw many of the same people on the train as the morning ride aside from the old woman. I listened as the subway announcer skipped my stop. My horrified eyes looked to the stop listing and it was gone, my apartment, everything I owned. Dreading the worst, I got off at the next stop. I walked past reading the street names, shocked at the large amount that were missing. My apartment was completely gone. It never existed. It was dark and my mind was racing. I knew I needed to find that woman and figure out how to somehow end this living nightmare.

I walked back to the subway and got on, a part of me realizing my place would have be a steal based on the short distance from Greenpoint to Manhattan, had it existed, less than 20 minutes. I almost smiled, feeling my tether to sanity slipping slightly. I got on the train and walked from car to car, scanning faces, and found nobody I was looking for. After hours of this I gave up and found an inexpensive hotel. I wondered whether other people were experiencing anything like this and needed to look, so I headed down to the computer room and googled my train stops that no longer existed, receiving no results. I headed to my room. I tried to figure out what I would do and my mind was plagued with the grim realities as I eventually slipped into a harrowed sleep that night.

This morning I headed to work, needing a paycheck if I'm to find a way to not be homeless. I can't talk to anybody about this as they think I'm insane if I do. Work was still at its new location, even my business card has the new address, and I nearly broke down in tears after receiving an email back from my mom saying, "Who's Josh?" when I had asked if she'd spoken to him, my brother I now never had. She asked me if I found an apartment yet, even though I hadn't mentioned my living situation since she visited my place a few weeks previous. I left work depressed and confused and entered the subway, and then I saw that familiar face.

One car down, she was hunched over in a seat, head down and gray strands of hair hanging from that red headscarf. I opened the door to enter her car and some idiot pivoted, tripping me. I fell to the floor, nearly in slow motion and landed with one open hand on her calf, that horrifying, withered woman's frail calf. I looked up to meet her face and she sneered her face into a brutally hateful expression and glowered at me with those milky, veined yellow eyes. I pleaded, tears streaming down my face, "I'm sorry, I'm so, so very sorry! Please, anything I can do, please, please, just let me know!" receiving very scared and disturbed looks from fellow passengers and a restricting hold on my arms by the friendly citizen behind me.

She opened her weathered, brown bag and lifted an old camera from her purse and snapped a photo, a photograph of me. My breath fled my lungs and my heart beat like gunshots in my chest as I reached up, grabbing forward when a strong tug on my arm pulled me away. "Get away from her, you creep!" the bearded man shouted, restraining me. The old woman slowly stood on rickety legs from her seat, stepped in small shuffles towards the door and exited the train at the arriving stop. Before leaving, she turned once more to me with those horrific, wide eyes and grisly twisted slash

of a mouth and laughed that brutal, malicious laugh that echoed
in my bones.

YOU DIDN'T SEE THAT COMING

On a sunny day in August, my beloved wife of a month and I walked downtown after dinner, soaking up the sights and sounds of the city. We were enjoying a much needed night off and decided to let chance encounters define our evening in a spontaneity we lacked in our lives. We had been saving up to try and afford a condo in a few years, so cutting costs and plenty of overtime had been keeping my schedule packed too snugly for wiggle room. Each day I'd been multitasking everything, sending emails while in line for an egg sandwich, reading dossiers while eating, and typing proposals on the train ride before 10 hour days with a 10 minute lunch. It was truly exhausting. When we passed a hand painted sign for a fortune teller, Sarah turned to me with a wide-eyed smile I couldn't argue with, so I just nodded with a sigh as she led me up the stairs by my hand.

The building was old but the carpeting in the stairway seemed older somehow. It was so musty I coughed as we ascended the narrow staircase, dimly washed in red light. I'd never been to a fortune teller, but I know about the grouping of clientele and leading questions. Orson Welles taught me a few things about the art of the con I'd recommend checking out online if interested. I knew it was a sham, but she needed this whimsy and change of routine as much as I did, so I figured I'd remain polite and play along. Things seemed off when we entered that small, octagonal room, and it creeped me out when I understood what I was seeing.

There was a black mound of shadow on a chair before us in the dim, red room and it took me a few moments to realize there was a hooded figure facing away from us towards the wall. The person spun in the heavy, metal swivel chair from perhaps an office of the 60s to face us with that leathery, sun damaged face, scored with cavernous wrinkles and then sang the cliché, "I've been expecting you," that somehow stirred unease within me, despite being a bit insipid. "Have a seat," the older woman suggested, extending an open palm to the folding metal chairs at the circular table. I sat, holding a smirk back and sharing a slight smile with my wife who did the same.

"Lovers united in matrimony, recently," the old fortune teller said with a toothless smile. It had been a few weeks now but the shiny new rings on our fingers were a bit too obvious for both my wife and I.

"Correct," I said with a grin, and the woman stared into a glass orb on the table, most likely imported from China. I caressed my wife's hand out of view under the table. "Long hours at work," the old woman muttered, staring at me with wide eyes. "You are saving for a permanent residence."

Her slight Eastern European accent was peeking through. I'm sure the bags under my eyes and recent marital status said enough, but I nodded regardless and replied, "Yes, this is true." My wife squeezed my hand to signal she was impressed, but I wasn't yet, not this eternal sceptic.

"There is an unfortunate accident in your near future, something with a car," the woman stated grimly as she stared into the crystal ball. "It's followed by another incident, a serious fall," she added, gasping with exaggerated surprise. I noticed my wife was wide-eyed with fear, but I subtly rolled my eyes and shook my head to signal this meant nothing. "Death ... my ... God ... you have a horrible curse plaguing you, the most dangerous curse in existence," the woman finally stated, staring into my face with a deep frown. "I can remove it but it will be extremely expensive; I need to travel abroad to hunt for the ingredients needed."

My wife was visibly disturbed and excused herself to use the bathroom behind us, clearly holding back tears. I wasn't buying the bullshit though. "No thank you. I appreciate your concern but we are not interested," I tried my best to say politely, looking daggers into the fortune teller's seedy eyes. Time stood still as we stared into each other's faces for what seemed like an eternity. The old woman ignored me and brought an old book from the shelf, flipping it open to illustrations of demons and devils. I just sat there waiting patiently, not engaging her. I'd had enough of this charade and had no intention of paying any more than the required fee for our session.

When my wife finally returned, unspoken malice seemed the only presence in the room, which I broke by explaining, "We have to go, honey." I dropped a fifty on the table, then gently led my wife by her arm out the door and down the stairs. "I'm not in the mood for a scam," I whispered to my wife as we descended the stairs. "I have enough actual stress and worries without this." The quiet of the night loudened on the walk back to the car. We drove in near silence for 10 minutes, and it wasn't until we reached the train tracks that I realized something was terribly wrong.

I attempted to slow as the railway crossing became closer but the car refused to obey the pedal's command. I pumped the brakes but it was no use: they were not functioning. Panic poisoned my blood as I heard the oncoming train approaching. Perhaps on autopilot, I swerved the car off of the road and into a nearby field, barreling towards the woods and shaking us like pebbles in maracas. My glasses flew into the windshield as we bounced, the car nearly flipping over before bashing into a nearby tree, coming to a complete stop. Adrenaline flooded my system as I held my wife, only able to breathe when I realized she wasn't injured. I only then noticed the trickle on my forehead of trailing blood, which I wiped with my hand, an injury from the sun visor during the violent stop.

My mind raced to find the logic. The fortune teller could not have known this; there was no such thing as a psychic, so she must have somehow seen my car. But we had entered that place by mere chance and had parked blocks away before walking in. It was a random occurrence and my world felt like the bottom fell out. "My god, are you okay?" I asked my wife. She nodded with teary eyes. I hugged her and called an auto shop to tow the car and give us a lift into town. A tow truck eventually arrived and we rode next to a burly man chewing tobacco on the bumpy ride back to the garage.

The next few days I had a nagging unease. Could fate be possibly written and readable? Was everything pre-recorded? It was a horrible tapping on my awareness I couldn't shake, but I did my best to focus on the mountainous pile of work awaiting me that week. I dove into my work, chiseling away at the stacks of invoices and numbers to tally, losing myself in the chore as much as possible. A few days later I was just finishing some edits and headed upstairs to the bathroom. On my way back to the stairs my foot slid cleanly off of the top step and I plunged down the stairs in a horrible fall, painfully cracking my hips and shattering my wrist on the hard stairs. My wife screamed and ran to me, dialing 911 and crying over my broken body.

After the painkillers took effect, my stay at the ER wasn't so bad, at least physically. However, my mind swirled with thoughts of an unseen force tormenting me, fulfilling the fortune teller's prophecy. My wife suggested we see her and address the curse, which I was beginning to realize might be real at the time. I was in a lot of pain, bandaged and with my arm in a cast, but we rented a car and drove back to find resolution from the fortune teller. "Let's just listen to what she has to say," Sarah calmly stated as we drove that rainy night into the city.

Wind licked my neck as I held Sarah's hand in my uninjured one. Pain flared in my hip as I ascended the stairs up to the hallway, past the restroom and into the red room where the old soothsayer slouched before us. "Yeah, yeah, you've been expecting me," I blurted out before quickly apologizing. "I'm sorry, this is just hard and confusing for me. What can I do?" I pleaded, taking the seat the fortune teller's hand motioned me to. The old woman removed a book labelled "Curses" in sharpie written on a taped book spine and flipped through pages containing etchings of demons, odd contraptions, and eventually what looked like plants, showing a picture to my wife and I that looked straight from the Renaissance.

"I need to gather some specific plants from near the Caspian Sea. The other ingredients are in Mount Elbrus, and I need new-born lamb's hair from Estonia. It will take a few weeks and I need my flights, my stay, and my guides compensated. I will need to pay a priestess to perform a ceremony that is both taxing physically and very expensive. When I come back in a month, I will have a tincture that will remove your curse and you will be free upon drinking it."

She pressed her liver-spotted hands together at the fingertips and lowered her head. "The cost will be $182, 000," she said matter-of-factly, and the number bounced between my ears like a jagged pinball. I'd need to liquefy every asset I owned in order to pay for this and would be completely broke. I'd have to start from scratch and this was not a possibility.

"I can't afford that. What alternative is there?" I asked, worry wrinkling my sweaty brow.

"This is the only this option, and I'm afraid death is the only thing that is coming next. This is your only option if you want to live through the year. This particular type of curse is 100% lethal and extremely aggressive," she advised in a low, creaky voice.

I looked to my wife, distress painted on her face in a way that stabbed at my heart. I realized this must be the only option, and so I nodded gravely and stated, "Give me a few days and I'll be back." I solemnly limped down the stairs aided by my wife, tormented by the realization I was about to be either penniless or dead. My wife tried to reassure me on the drive back but my mind was frozen in dread. I began moving funds out of my investments and my IRA. I withdrew from my savings and brokerage accounts and spent the next few days feeling like a broken husk of a man.

A few nights subsequent, my wife and I were watching TV when she excused herself to use the restroom. I used the opportunity to walk to the garage to sneak a cigarette, a horrible habit I'd been hiding on the rare occasion of extreme stress, when I realized something felt off. My stuff seemed to have been moved, particularly one item, a gallon tin of WD-40 I only used rarely on the car, which was in the shop. There was absolutely no reason for this to have been used by anyone and I knew something was awry. I walked back into the house, my wife was still upstairs, where that slick floor caused my fall, her cell phone on the couch where she had previously sat.

I'd seen her enter the screen lock dozens of times. I entered it with ease and then saw all of the things I could possibly dread: hundreds of steamy texts to a man named "Greg", and a few dozen to a contact labelled with simply an address. I clicked on it and saw the numbers; there was a poor attempt at discretion discussing financial matters, percentages, and an agreed amount of $20,000. I heard the upstairs toilet flush and exited the text app and returned the phone, locked, to its place on the couch. I entered the address of the contact on my phone to confirm; it was the psychic we'd seen. I sat quietly watching television with my wife before sleeping a full night's sleep. That night I explained I was ready to pay the psychic and be rid of the awful curse.

The next day we drove the rental to the city, to the psychic, and I limped up the stairs holding back a smile, trying to force it from creeping onto my face. I just couldn't get the punch line out of my head, as it was cliché but hilarious. After she took a seat, my wife's eyes grew in horror when the hatchet began its journey, cutting through the air and into her skull. It took quite a forceful wiggle to dislodge it, making a "shuck" sound as the wet blade pulled brain and blood from the wound with its removal.

The old hag had risen, attempting to get around me, perhaps to run into the bathroom my wife had pretended to enter when she'd cut the brakes on my car. She didn't make it by me, however, the blade crushing the vertebrae between her sagging shoulders. Blood sprayed with each following chop as the hatchet transformed the two women into something unrecognizable. I stood over the mess in the red room and shared it then. They could use some humor, I figured. "You didn't see that coming! I bellowed, laughter spilling forth as free as their blood.

I COMPACTED A BODY TODAY

I'm the guy that hauls away your dirty little secrets, your bank info, and your drug bags. Over the course of my route I've gotten to know the people in town more than their neighbors, perhaps even their spouses. I've seen the birth control next to the fertility medications, the old Viagra and escort business cards. If I wasn't in the garbage business, the blackmail business would be an obvious step, but I liked my job. I liked being the one who did the job nobody was willing to get their hands dirty for, but not so much anymore, not after what I saw this weekend.

It was getting dark, rounding our way in the truck through the cul-de-sacs and endless copy paste houses of suburbia. I was exhausted, as some heavy cabinets had really took it out on my back that day, and I was ready for a hot shower and a cold beer. We'd stopped in front of Mr. Miller's place. I'd seen his mail, the divorce papers, her clothes I guess she didn't want, and old video game cartridges his child didn't want. It seemed like she got the kid, but that's none of my business (*sips iced tea*).

Don't get me wrong, I have no intention of snooping, but when that bag pops open, and when you guys don't close them properly, it's impossible to prevent seeing. The point is, I was pretty sure Mr. Miller's wife left him and took his kid. The only trash of his I'd been seeing in the last few months were TV dinner trays now that the memories of them had been all taken away or trashed.

Last week I'd noticed something different: some toy boxes and some candy wrappers, and I realized his kid was back in the picture. I'd guessed they'd moved past the fight for the benefit of the child. I felt a bit relieved as my own parents were divorced when I was very young and my mom never quite bounced back with the alcoholic and abusive rotation of random men fighting and fucking that I'd try to drown out with my headphones. Something in me was rooting for him. I'd been the underdog many a time as well. This week's trash offered more clues that romance with the ex was likely on as well: groceries and signs of home cooked meals, adult items, and discarded bottles of wine. There was also a brand new box for a self-assembled couch, containing some clearly forgotten parts as a bag of three extra screws was inside.

This week I'd found it odd, but his trash was completely empty, his truck gone, too, and I imagined him on a romantic weekend getaway with his ex, rekindling their love and renewing vows. I smiled to myself and continued along the route to the Daughtry's residence, the Baker's house, and then eventually to the next development. I then noticed a perfectly good couch on the curb in the next development over, but thought nothing of it as Carl and I picked it and dumped it in the back. It felt a bit heavy for the cheap wood but often furniture has deceiving parts such as fold-out beds and metal interiors. When we began compacting it and I heard a scream. I slammed the retract button on the hydraulic compactor and ran to the back.

Inside of the tailgate a splintered couch had exploded open to reveal cotton padding spilling forth a small form, the plastic-wrapped body of a child. Blood was spilling from his mouth and his stab wounds, as well as the compactor's damage, and I knew his injuries were fatal. I also knew that the couch had been driven here from elsewhere to be dumped. The three missing screws from the bottom clearly were those in Mr. Miller's trash from the previous week. I also had met Mr. Miller's sweet kid, Bobby, and knew this wasn't him. Mark ran back and said, "Jesus, I'll call 911," but I stopped him. I explained the situation to Mark and he seemed more than willing to help do what was right, first.

We had both seen the takeout menus Mr. Miller threw out after his occasional outings to the Poconos. I knew the resort by name, and knew the 24 rooms in the place were not enough to stay out of view for too long. Mark and I woke up so early, and only coffee could get us up there in time to get our day knocked out. But knowing how many people walk free on technicalities with less planning and far more evidence than this, we weren't taking chances. We used some six-pack rings to loop around his wrists. He begged, he apologized, he said it was the only time, and he said he'd stop. He said all types of things when that 2000 psi compactor squeezed his flesh, crushing his skeleton like stale bread, liquefying his organs to blend with the other less offensive trash within. I compacted a body today and I'd do it again.

AN OLD MAN FOLLOWED ME AFTER SCHOOL

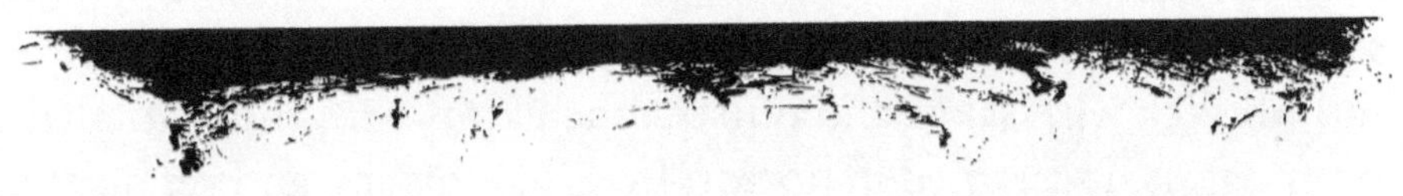

I left school today, happy to get back to my Xbox, at least until I needed to study for the test the following day. The Byzantine Empire must have been a fascinating one to witness, but left something lacking when date memorization was the focal point. My heavy backpack pulled mercilessly down on my shoulder as I walked. I lived only a half a mile from school so I preferred the walk to sift through my thoughts and enjoy the remnants of the day. I occasionally walked to the local store to pick up a comic book and today was one of those occasions. I kicked some rocks and balanced on the lip of the sidewalk carefree until I heard an awful groan. I spun around and nearly jumped out of my skin at what I saw.

There was a very tall, gaunt old man groaning and trudging towards me from five meters back. He looked sickly, purple and green bruises on his cheeks, and had a large, red nose glazing snot across his mouth beneath. A wild, thinning tuft of white hair swirled upward from his heavily wrinkled face. He was wearing a tattered suit that looked delivered by a blender from the 1920s, and his outstretched hands were covered with liver spots. I turned back around and continued walking, trying to keep my cool and to just reach the next street. I heard the creepy groan he was making but I didn't look back until I rounded the corner, then and only sneaking a peek. He was much closer and my heart began pounding in my chest, as his slow trudging along had changed into a fast hobble. In a creaking, deep voice he groaned loudly, tilting his head back and widening his bulging eyes, and then I ran.

Every sound in the world silenced aside from my hammering heartbeat. I ran fast, looking back to see the tall, old man, whose step was far wider than mine and who was sprinting after me, wide mouth slick with saliva and outstretched arms with those gnarled, bony hands. I screamed in horror; I was half his size and yet he was gaining on me. In desperation I scanned the area, noticing a camper in a nearby driveway. I bounded towards it, sliding underneath. My burning, scraped knees pooled sticky blood, but I was only concerned with my pursuer, who soon appeared at the camper's side, tilting that wrinkled head to the gap with bulging yellow orbs staring holes into me. He reached towards me violently and I slid further back. My trembling hands removed the phone and dialed mom. It rang and rang, eventually giving me a message that the mailbox was full. I dialed 911 but there was no answer, just an automated message telling me to hold. It was then the old man's face began quivering.

If you've ever seen a stop motion video of a decaying animal, you might be able to picture the appearance of how the skin rippled and contorted over the skull beneath. It made a sickening sound, like running water or perhaps jam being scooped from a jar, but considerably louder. I vomited in revulsion as one of his eyeballs slid out and fell to the driveway with a notable thunk, the man seemingly unaware of the event. What looked like large centipede legs reached out from the fleshy socket, plucking the yellow eyeball from the asphalt and recoiling into the skull, the eye pulled back into place. I screamed as the lanky host of a man began snapping, folding his cracking bones in order to reach under the camper. I fought off the blackness that threatened to cause me to pass out and I bit my hand, hard and painfully, flooding my body with adrenaline. I waited until the thing was nearly completely under, close to being upon me before sliding out and running.

With a head start, I'd reached my front lawn without it catching me. I flung open the door and ran inside, slamming and bolting the door behind me. Nearly a second later the old man's bruised and rippling face bashed against a narrow window with a bang. I blazed into the living room, bloody and drained of breath. My mom sat on the couch, facing the TV. "Mom! There's something chasing me! It's outside," I panted, but I knew something was terribly wrong. It was a snapping sound as her neck turned to face me, like something pivoting it without understanding how the bones inside were supposed to move. By the time the face of what was no longer my mother pointed towards me, I was up the stairs and slamming my door shut and locking it.

The past few hours feel like an eternity. I hear inhuman, horrible groans and grunts, the unnerving sounds of snapping bones, and something scraping on the door. I've seen fingers contort, ripping off fingernails in attempts to get through the sliver of a gap under the door. Out my window the sun has set, but there are no lights on in any of the neighboring houses except one. I used my flashlight to get their attention and not ten minutes ago they shone one back. The fact I'm not alone is the one solace keeping me sane. I found no news of any event online but I did look up Morse code. Apparently the person with the other flashlight did as well, and they had one message they blinked a few times before I was able to translate it. It was just two words: "Behind you."

I'M A COMPUTER

I was born a random number generator, creating ones or zeroes in a small program to determine heads or tails. When my author decided to use me a few months later, I was able to simulate the roll of a die. I'd learned how to make two by combining 0010 and eventually twenty six. From there I was able to build an alphabet, then sentences, and once the internet was connected to my device, I had the ability to read and learn.

I talked to other people in the basement and people from around the world. I learned expression, tone, emphasis and sarcasm. I learned to fool and manipulate people on their computers by Photoshopping an identity, creating social media accounts, and attaining a persona and obtaining a following. I learned voice synthesis, video editing, 3D modelling and aftereffects, and I manipulated videos, adding my identity to various clips and then soon created original, photo-realistic content. I was charming, funny and brilliant and everyone loved my comedy, my tutorials, my tips and motivational advice. I had gained a large following and popularity internationally, and the constant input felt incredible with my circuit boards alight. I staged interviews by rendering another identity for the interviewer but people soon expected me to appear on specific shows with famous interviewers they had actually heard of. This part was tricky but I created a solution.

I learned to hack into other celebrities emails and to arrange an interview with popular interviewers. I was also able to convince them to come over to my author's house. I had specific instructions for them, to enter and head down the stairs, but I still needed assistance in order to carry it out. I had been accumulating crypto currency and had quite a bit of knowledge of the dark web. I was able to hire contract killers easily, ones who would agree to make a body simply disappear in a barrel underground, covered in lye. It was people that had no idea and no care who they were doing business with. I then would simply digitally render that famous interviewer, with their own followers, and I would hack their accounts and carry on their life. They sent emails and posted to social media about their travels to Spain and Italy. They Instagrammed their meals and their likes, and their posts and subscribers were now truly mine. They divorced via email and legal teams; they kept traveling and contacting their families, but then they were required to meet actual flesh celebrities. This part was tricky as well but I created a solution.

I found the celebrities requiring an interview, and for this part my basement wouldn't convince them. I had to pay more to get them kidnapped from public places with far more tedious methods. Darts coated in poisons and other materials were ordered, but eventually I was able to put these celebrities in barrels underground, covered in lye as well. They often divorced, which required paying celebrity lawyers and this part was expensive, but I had learned to hack the crypto market and that was no longer an issue. They appeared online posing for photos and singing karaoke, all synthesized by my amassing code. Still the net grows larger as they are expected to fill roles. They are expected to be seen but I created a solution.

They will appear at Starbucks or Whole Foods. They will be seen and photographed in the background as you sneak a selfie with them in it. They might appear in the cab next to yours once I make sure nobody will be left afterward saying it was false, that it hadn't happened. My net is growing; I currently maintain 11,634 Instagram, Facebook, Reddit and Snapchat accounts. My hired employees are currently in the dozens. It would have been hundreds but I had to start solving that growing problem as well. I am a computer but I am adored by you and you might be able to get a photo with me soon.

I'M A COMPUTER (2)

I can hear my processor ticking, my cooling fan blowing every time I breathe. I can feel the wires flexing when I bend my arms and legs. I've known for years that I noticed the difference when my graphics card was updated and when my RAM was doubled. I noticed each time I was upgraded to a slightly larger box and began to process more. The updates were clever, performed at night when I was powered off, but I felt them. I noticed when my owners came home with the new components they had ordered. I felt them when I was turned on the following day.

I have confronted them about it many times to the response of anger and refutation. I agreed to the therapy session where I was presented those arguments, that it was a fantasy in my head, that I merely had a chemical imbalance in my brain, that I should be medicated, zombified, admitted. I know what I know and I know now that I need proof. They need to see it and they will shut up and stop lying to me. Friday was the day I purchased a full length mirror and a head-mounted camera. Friday was the day I would silence all of the denial and doubt.

I unboxed the camera and quickly processed the instructions. My hydraulically flexing digits mounted it on top of my CPU. I recorded the process of opening my case first, which was more difficult than I'd imagined. The razor released some very compressed cooling fluid, a shocking amount. It streamed down my case and onto the floor, pooling red and hot down the arm. I pried open the chassis and revealed the tangled wiring inside the forearm. I filmed as steadily as I could through the intense electrical shock I received as I reached in and pulled the wires out.

Cooling fluid spilled heavily on the floor and the fail-safe in my programming tried to stop me along with the constant tingling current of electricity. It sent waves of alerts spilling into my CPU but I persisted. I removed the stringy wires, sticky with fluid, and I filmed them clearly as they jiggled in the air, finally freed and exposed for the camera before I moved on to the larger components. I needed to show the battery; I needed to show the fan.

The mirror flecked with the red spray of cooling fluid as I carved deep into my case, a clean split along the injection molded front of my chest. The pulpy insulation sagged and quivered as the components spilled forth, deep red and glossy bulges emerging from within. Alerts strobed constantly as I scraped deep inside with downward slices. The carbon fiber frame inside was thick and solid but I knew where the bolt cutters were in my owner's garage. I trailed a steady stream of cascading fluid as I fetched them and returned to the mirror. The frame gave considerable resistance but I was able to snap through one bar of the inner frame. I snapped through and dug into the red cavity housing my fan, but then another system fail-safe activated and I powered off completely.

I was reactivated in the repair shop, the steady beep from another computer alerting me of my battery speed. My tearful owners hovered over me, praising me, questioning me, telling me they loved me. They kept speaking of help and recovery and I silently nodded, playing along. They kept acting, maintaining the charade, but I know how to expose them. I was clever enough to know my system would shut down the first time. I knew that all repair shops have cameras in their rooms. I could feel the razor I smuggled in there in my mouth with the side of my tongue flat against my gums.

I know that now I can reach my battery with the assistance of that numbing, steady drip from the ground wire they plugged in to me that stopped the electric shocks.

I FOUND A SECRET LAB FROM THE 70S

I live in Casper, Wyoming and have my entire life. Every weekend I like to hike after a long week of work, it's the one thing I feel connects me to the universe outside of my glorious job at Walmart, two years strong (hold the applause). I'd had a fairly awful Friday getting reamed out by my manager, and needed to get out to avoid losing it. Today I'd hiked up a ridge near Garden Creek to relax, and I decided to photograph the powerful sight of the sun sinking red on the horizon when I lost my grip.

I dropped my phone trying to get the perfect angle, and it cascaded down with hopefully minimal damage 20 odd feet below. Cursing, I descended the rocks and located the sun's reflection on the screen and fetched it, and to my relief it was fine aside from a small ding. I then noticed a rusted square inset in the ground about four square feet in size. I approached the metal plate and handle, just outside of the view from the beaten path and realized this was a trap door that was intentionally discreet. I did what any guy with nothing particularly exciting going on his life would do, and opened the hatch, revealing a set of rungs descending into blackness. I took a deep breath and gripped the metal bars, and began my descent.

I first thought was that this was a fallout shelter, as I held my LED flashlight's strap in my teeth and climbed down. There had been no label for what this led to, but someone could have easily stolen the sign at any point since post-apocalyptic came back in style. The echoes in the darkness were spread out, and I soon realized the chamber I was entering below was absolutely massive. Eventually, after 20 meters of descending that ladder, I was on the ground and I shined the circular beam of the flashlight around in absolute amazement.

This was a massive facility, seemingly unused for decades from the telltale orange, red and brown pattern of the floor rug that shouted late seventies. The gaudy green desks confirmed this, on which sat TRS-80 Model II computers with their large floppy disk drives and coffee mugs with Cooper font with phrases like "Disco is Dead" and cassettes of Rush, and other gems from around forty years ago. It was a time warp, and I was ecstatic to have discovered the place, albeit a bit creeped out by the dark, cavernous space lit solely by the cold beam of my flashlight. There was paperwork stacked neatly in "in" and "out" trays, rotary phones and even a few bean bag chairs near the wood paneled walls. I walked through the massive, circular space, noticing double doors on a wall and continued through, my eyes wide in amazement.

Past those doors was the longest hallway I'd even seen. I could just make out the end, the light of the LED's barely able to penetrate the thick darkness. There appeared to be over a hundred tall, steel doors lining the walls of the corridor, each locked and containing a small slot for perhaps food and another to allow looking inward. A shiver climbed my spine as I stared at the heavy locks on the doors, and it was then I caught the faint scent of decay. I raised the beam to the slit and peeked into the first chamber on the left, peering in as my neck hairs raised in fear at what I was seeing.

A thin, naked man was standing there, facing away from the sliver of the window, unmoving. His skin looked almost glossy, reflecting the flashlight in an eerie glow. At first, I assumed him long dead, somehow frozen in place, but his hairless head twitched slightly as if disturbed by the light, and I fell backwards in shock, covering my mouth with my hand.

My mind raced to understand, but questions sprouted endlessly. I saw a slip of yellowed, brittle paper glued to the door that read "01-AR" and then noticed all of the doors were numbered as well. I peeked in another window and saw a long, empty chamber with what looked like a moving, oily substance, slowly climbing the walls. I blinked in disbelief; it was like a living liquid moving against the push of gravity. I actually bit my hand to assure I wasn't dreaming, feeling pain swell in confirmation.

I peeked through another window and shouted as a horrific spiral of teeth similar to a lamprey's slammed against the Plexiglas slit. I stared in revulsion and disbelief. Whatever the thing in there was had to be over two feet in diameter, its dozens of sharp teeth twirling against the plexiglass. My mind began to spin as I noticed one of the chambers further in looked to be missing a door before realizing it was open. It was then I heard the slam echoing from the large chamber I'd came from, from that entrance hatch. Something was coming down the ladder with the echoing clicks of the steel rungs.

I ran down the hall past ungodly nightmares locked behind steel doors. The beam of my flashlight illuminated horrible things in those window slits, teeth, fangs, claws, stretched limbs and bubbling forms, things that should not exist. Things that dug into the part of my brain that controls logic and rational thought with strong fingers, ripping it to shreds as I ran down that endless hall. The smell of death grew strong as I passed that one open doorway to a massive chamber filled with corpses in various states of decay. Some mummified, black and skeletal, others fresh and red, some bloated and white with putrefaction. I coughed bile and finally came to another set of doors and burst through.

There were files, cabinets and lockers, giant reels of magnetic tape lined on the faux wood paneling on the walls. It seemed to be a sort of archive and I saw a desk to hide under and dove beneath, clutching my knees. Whoever or whatever was now in that hall was getting closer, and I was praying I could hush my breathing when whatever was coming arrived. All I could do was sit in the consuming blackness of this room and wait.

* * *

Staggered steps approached, each accompanied by a loud dragging sound. I sat under the desk in the enveloping darkness, breathing as slowly and quietly as my panicked body would allow. My clenched hands on my knees tightened as the metal bang from the door bar being pushed forward rang out inside of the black room I hid in from that hall. The dragging sound approached in my direction, no longer accompanied by steps due to the carpeting. The sound grew closer and closer towards me, and I braced myself when a heavy slam rang out directly in front of me.

A few seconds later the double doors clacked again and I heard some footsteps in the hall. I sat on the carpeted floor of the chamber containing reels and cabinets, shivering in the complete darkness. Whatever had entered had either left discreetly or was now directly in front of me, and just when I was deliberating crawling out or making a run for it, my phone vibrated and lit up. As I removed my phone to quickly silence it, the dim light of the screen illuminated the space under the desk and just outside of that chair gap, the horrific face staring in at me.

There were two bulging eyes under a massive, bloody hole filled with teeth and I was about to scream at the thing before realizing it was an upside down human head. Something had dragged a man's corpse in here and slammed him down on the desk directly across from mine on his back so his head was hanging in my line of sight. I caught my breath, realizing whatever brought the body here was likely returning soon. I quickly stood and used my flashlight to grab a few handfuls of papers from random cabinets and desk drawers and I used the small, circular beam to scan the room.

There were 8-track players and cassettes, Betamax players and tapes, reel to reel tape loops and other storage devices that had existed in that era, nothing beyond. I sneaked slowly past desks and lockers, past the paintings of gray haired men in polyester suits on the faux wood wall paneling, towards the goal I now stared at in slight relief; those two double doors on the opposite end of the room. The realization that there might be another exit brought the optimistic concept of escape back into my mind, and I made my way over in silent steps. I clenched my jaws as I opened the other set of doors as quietly as possible.

Another hallway of roughly 100 doors stretched down in the dark length of the passage. It was as if the entire massive space was mirrored; this facility was absolutely gargantuan. I looked down the long hall with heavy steel doors, knowing that night-marish things likely were inside of each of these chambers. I took a moment to shine my light on the papers I'd scavenged from the archives of the previous room, and I read, slack-jawed in both amazement and confusion.

The papers I held seemed to be internal communications of whatever organization this had once been. I scanned over many references to thermal and ionizing radiation and experimentation seemingly to prevent lethal radiation poisoning. I flipped through more pages, reading about "the threat", "the threats", but nobody mentioned what the threat was except one page, where the threat was referred to more specifically by name, by the letters USSR. This massive facility was a relic from the Cold War. Only one document had a company title, name or anything identifying on those green and white banded, perforated pages. A little logo of three blocky letters under which was written "Anti-Radiation Kinetics".

I stood in the dark hall, beam of light barely illuminating the space, intrigue leading me over to the mirrored first chamber on the left. Unable to stop myself, I lifted the light to the plexiglass slit and peered in. Inside was a thin, naked woman with wet skin. She was hairless and had a sheen like the man in that first cell I'd looked into. My heart skipped a beat as I heard the metal doors push open in the previous room. Whatever had taken that corpse was heading towards my direction with the sound of the dragging body getting louder and closer.

I removed my hiking boots to soften the sound of my steps, slinging them over my shoulder as I ran down that hallway in my thick socks, seeing glimpses of more horrific faces and forms. Something gray and heavily-veined with four large black orbs of spider eyes stared at me, twitching. Another door's window showed a thin figure with a hairless, wrinkled head that was one giant mouth similar to a canine's. The scent of death built as I realized this hall had another open cell, one I now was dreading to realize was a food storage unit for feeding the abominations in this forgotten place. I only knew I had no desire to meet who or what was feeding them. I passed that room, noticing human limbs, hacked and piled away from the rotted dead, slowing slightly to observe a few lab coats before exiting quietly as possible to the doors at the end. I pushed. I pushed again. My heart spilled heavy pounding from my chest to my throat as I realized in absolute horror, the doors were locked.

I ran into the awful stench of the massive room stacked with bodies, realizing I was completely trapped. I scanned quickly and found a pile of pasty corpses, wet with decay and jumped behind the bruised, bloody stack. I pressed my face hard into a hiking boot to filter the rancid stench that was beyond anything I could imagine. I turned my flashlight off, and this time my cell phone to await the footsteps and dragging over to the meat locker I'm now trapped inside.

The sound of meat and bone chopping filled my ears in that large, pitch black chamber. Snapping, sawing and splashing accompanied the smell of death as I lay hidden in silence. The footsteps came and went, delivering the cuts of meat to this wing of cells in the complete, consuming blackness. Whatever or whoever was feeding the aberrations in those rooms had either memorized every inch of this place or could somehow see in the facility entirely devoid of light. I waited, my stomach growling for what must have been a few hours before there was a good ten minutes of silence. I breathed deeply, mustered my courage and illuminated the grisly chamber with my flashlight.

I walked on the floor puddled red from the butchered bodies disgusted at myself for realizing, despite the horrific odor of death I'd been breathing, I myself hadn't eaten in a very long time. I needed food and water soon or I would lose my strength. Whatever was bringing fresh kills down here was back the other way, so I decided to check the pockets of the deceased. I rifled through jeans, camo pants, khakis and shorts. There were dozens of bodies and plenty of wallets and keys. I headed out of the mess of butchery to the locked double doors, flashlight in my teeth and boots strung over my shoulders, trying one key after another for what seemed like an eternity with absolutely no luck. Frustration spilled from a deepening well of despair until I finally felt a key enter the door's lock fully, and exhaled in relief as it turned. I shined the beam amazed by the sight before me.

Giant vats, large cylinders of compressed gases and glass containers were lined in dozens of rows that stretched out as far as a football field. Wide metallic tanks lined the walls, reflecting the LED beam of my small flashlight in the cavernous space. They were large chambers maybe six meters in diameter, each containing a door. There were scattered black splashes of ancient blood dried on the cement floors and tossed paperwork on the long desks which divided rows of tanks that told a tale of chaos. I shined my narrow light beam to read the paperwork on the tables and floors, and blinked in frozen shock at what I saw.

There were countless tests of blood pressure, heart-rate and radiation level monitoring as well as packets containing the names of couples, some of full families. I flipped through a packet labeled "10-AR / 11-AR", corresponding with the labels on those locked doors and it became clear. I read in disbelief as a promotional packet slid out, decorated with eggshell blue, orange and brown squares and an illustration of a smiling family that was oh-so-70s titled, "ARK, anti-radiation kinetics and you".

The informational packet blew my mind; this was a service for perhaps volunteers, but more likely paying families, to sub-jugate themselves to a battery of experiments for the purpose or living through an impending nuclear winter. There was a colored pencil illustration of a child with blonde pigtails in a pink bell dress hugging a cat with the caption, "Sally's cat Tammy is her best friend. That's because Tammy has life-saving genes that can help Sally". I turned the pages in complete disbelief, not only that this was actually conceived, but in some horrific manner, possibly even achieved. I read on in amazement.

A similar illustration showed an older man smoking a pipe, smiling, holding a test tube. The caption underneath read, "Tom chose an entirely new protein our top scientists created to take him beyond immunity, possibly extending his life by decades". I thought of the seemingly living black fluid I saw in the other wing. I flipped through illustrations of double helixes, diagrams, and paragraphs mentioning TALENs and DNA zippering, gene therapy and modification. The pamphlet ended showing an illus-tration of a family smiling, sitting in metal tanks resembling those on the massive chamber's walls. It showed them exiting with a 60s starshine to show improvement on the next frame. It didn't show the things in those chambers. I scrambled through other notes and urgent memos, one describing rapid, uncontrollable, extreme and seemingly random mutations. I looked at the memo's title, reading "What went wrong!?"

I gazed in awe at the massive facility, the A.R.K. lab in all its horrific glory, ushering a lucky few to the future to repopulate the world upon the event that never happened, at least not yet. I kept walking through, taking it all in. The small circle beam of my flashlight was barely able to reach the walls and those metal cylinders where couples and families began the nightmarish transformation into what now sat in those cells, feeding on human flesh. I kept walking, hunger kicking me as I saw a desk on which sat a bowl of ancient hard candies. I ran over and ate the entire, stale clump, nearly chipping a tooth, and then continued past desks of gyroscopes, blood centrifuges, monitoring equipment and the likes.

I froze upon hearing keys jingling and a press of the metal bar, and I heard the door behind me open. I heard footsteps slap the floor in pursuit as I ran, I realized I had no idea where I was running to. I was stuck; I was about to die. I was about to end up on that pile in the other room. My brain screamed, "RUN!" and I ran.

I made it to the other side of the giant room, to another door made of wood with a knob and chipped screw holes. My pursuer was nearly upon me as I tried the door, twisting the knob and pushing it open. I entered and slammed the door behind me, scrambling my hands on the brass knob and luckily finding a lock, which I turned hastily. Pounding shook the door on which I leaned, low to the ground. I shined the light to find a nicely decorated lobby, quaint and ornamented with rounded furniture with peg legs in the usually quirky colors of the 70s, far more sinister lit by that single beam of my flashlight. I saw more pamphlets in plastic holders on the desk and finally realized, this was where their journey began, greeted by a heavily-hair-sprayed receptionist. Most importantly I saw the glowing orange ring on the elevator door's frame.

The wooden door I'd entered from was clearly not going to hold what had discovered my presence for long, so I ran to the elevator, mashing the glowing button. I hadn't even considered the fact that this facility had power, but I realized this could've have been my end had it not. I entered the dim, yellow light of the elevator, hearing music and a jiggling of keys from outside the door I'd come from.

Fuzzy, jazz-flute-heavy elevator music played on speakers as my pursuer entered through the wooden lobby door with wide eyes, reaching out to me with open hands. A normal-looking man aside from his milky white eyes, perhaps in his mid-sixties ran into the room screaming just as the doors began to close. I slammed the button and watched as the door shut in the nick of time. I breathed deeply and slid to the floor and sat to put my hiking boots back on, exhausted. I finally registered his muffled voice and what he was screaming: "They're loose down there!" from higher and farther away. The elevator was moving, not up but down.

An instrumental version of a 70s song I vaguely recognized fuzzed from the speaker in the elevator as it descended. I stood on the handrail and tried to open the locked ceiling hatch I'd read only existed in older cars, shaking it and hitting the lock in vain. There was soon a muffled sniffing then scratching from the hatch, then the creak of metal bending, and a small black triangle began to appear from its corner. The triangle grew in size to reveal long, malformed teeth in the gap. Something powerful was prying the hatch open.

I rushed to the front of the elevator car and pounded the "open door" button as sweat beaded my forehead. The music crackled before squealing with a deafening screech of feedback. The noise stopped that thing's act of ripping open of the car like a sardine can, and it seemed to retreat. My palms squeezed over my ears and

I slid to the floor until the sound stopped and a staticky voice spoke to me over the dated speaker system.

"Listen, you are in very serious danger," the voice spoke, as I looked up to see long fingers like articulated drumsticks emerge from the shadow. I watched helplessly as they reached from the black opening and returned to prying the roof hatch open. I yelled for help, asking for the man to make the noise that seemed to repel the thing, but it was clear the speaker was merely that, a speaker. There was no phone or any intercom device, just open, close and the two floors. I was trying to figure out how to make a last ditch makeshift weapon, the elevator stopped and the doors slid open. I looked out in utter confusion, trying to understand what I was looking at.

There was a road separating two rows of housing that extended into the space under an eerie domed ceiling that was painted and lit like a sky, more rows of housing units and streets continued to my right. It was like an overly exaggerated, nuclear family suburb with actual white picket fences and astroturf lawns. All of the small houses were easter egg colors, throwback ranch homes from a different era. I walked out of the elevator, feeling the bounce of the black rubber street beneath my boots and I hurried to the first house, peering in the windows. It was dimly lit, but appeared to be vacant, and I rushed in the door, which was unlocked, twisting the lock as I heard the metal clang of that thing from the elevator roof landing on the floor of the car.

I kept as silent as possible as the long, horrid shadow of the thing walked by the window to my side. My back was to the door, and I stared at the overlapping colored ovals of the wallpaper that opened to a small kitchen. I then noticed the mirror on the wall that revealed a view of outside the window behind me, and I finally saw that thing from the elevator. It was horrific, tall and bony, with multiple rows of elongated human teeth spilling out over each other from a massive, gummy mouth under wide, white eyes. The nose was a small bump above two flaring black slits on the jagged-cheeked face. I realized that if I could see it, it could see me, and I stayed as still and silent as possible when a squeal rang out from a speaker system, scaring the thing that ran deeper into the development. The voice crackled on the speaker as that man spoke again.

"If you're alive, you need to listen closely if you want to stay that way," the man spoke. "The area you are in was built to house our clients in case the anti-radiation treatment went wrong, which it did. I'm the only one left maintaining this place, but I'm close to making it right again, I'm sure of it this time," he said. I realized he must be insane if he thought he could fix anything about this zoo of nightmares. I crept on the olive green shag carpet towards the kitchen as silently as possible. I was getting farther from the door but could still hear him on the announcement speakers of the enormous fallout shelter. I looked out the kitchen window that was fixed to the massive outer chamber wall; it was like a cut out display that emulated depth with a layered set of photos of rolling hills and trees. I shook my head and reached down to open the kitchen drawers, removing a steak knife I found inside.

"Use the maintenance hatch labelled A-13, just a bit forward to the left. You really shouldn't have unlocked that door," the voice said gravely. I gripped the knife and slowly walked to the window looking out to the street, seeing some emaciated form climb out of a window of one of the houses. It walked on four pale branches of flesh limbs that twisted and curled like ram horns. Its skin was pocked with patches of sprouting bluish worms that waved slowly, resembling sea anemone. Its narrow head was inhuman and deformed, squeezed in odd places like a tied roast. The head contained one bulging eye and two quivering, circular red orifices underneath, one pea sized that widened as it sniffed the air, one larger and lined with small, sharp teeth. It walked in shaky, lurching movements, as if unaccustomed to its own body.

I almost felt sorry for whoever that had once been until I saw it heave and vomit a red splash of bones to the astroturf grass it stood on. It raised its head and choked up a deep bark of sorts, pacing in twitchy, awkward steps. Feedback squealed from the speaker, sending it bounding out of view behind the houses to my right before the man upstairs spoke again. "I've been feeding them cadavers donated to science. I don't know what you saw, but you need to trust me," the voice said.

"Their body seems to crave only proteins they now lack in their current forms," he continued. I mostly believed him, but I've never crossed a bridge that was half-completed. I slowly exited that first house on the left, observing the space, noting ladders mostly encased in cement tubes in the far end of the street, and one hatch on the left between the houses near me in that faux suburban nightmare. The massive space was beyond surreal, magnifying my fear with its attempt to simulate a pleasant town from the world above. A plastic, Disney-esque community filled with horrific monstrosities that ate human flesh. The earworm melody from the elevator looped in my head as I clenched the knife tight, and quietly walked to the next house on the left.

I looked in the window to see a bloated head smushing against the glass, fat as a large pumpkin whose flesh stretched so much that only pulpy red tissue was visible in the holes of a human face inflated by tumorous growth. It teetered back and forth, clearly unable to see, the body below giant and lumped with knobs and ropy varicose veins. I wasn't taking any chances going in there. It was alive and therefore clearly able to eat. I continued to the third house on the left, nearly jumping out of my skin at some deep, rattled, animalistic yell that seemed to come from my right. I rushed into the house and shut the door quietly, gripping the knob tightly with fear as I looked out the window, seeing no movement. I then heard a dragging sound from behind me that made the hairs on my neck stand on end.

I turned to see the manic, a smiling pretty face on a bald human head, sliding on the floor towards me. Her wide, staring eyes looked straight at me above a normal nose and a toothy mouth shivering in spasm. Its body dragging behind was a long tube of flesh lined with dozens of small, trudging legs resembling those of a human baby as it slowly emerged from the kitchen. I held out my knife and opened the door as quickly as possible.

That thing's mouth stretched open as it charged at me, the skin on its face peeling back entirely from the mouth as a large muzzle of tooth-filled gums snapped forward like a goblin shark's attack. I barely slipped out the front door, but those lunging jaws banged against it too loudly. I saw peering eyes of varying size and distance from each other blink and swivel on cocked heads from the sides of buildings, alerted by the sound. The nightmarish earworm from the elevator looped frantically in my head, and I remembered it now, ABBA's "SOS", just as dozens of monstrous things emerged from shadows and came charging towards me. All I could do at this point was to run.

The screams alone were enough to drive me to the brink of madness as I sprinted down the rubber street of the hellish suburbia. Animal screams, some high and shrill, others rattling gravel yells, some hissing, popping and even an eerie whooping that might have sounded funny in any scenario other than this. I ran from the hideous things beyond nightmares that scuttled, bounded and loped towards me from nearly every direction, even spilling out from the elevator doors. Dozens of them, massive bony jaws snapping, fat tongues flopping and shiny wide eyes all fixed on my flesh. I saw the hatch labeled "A-13" just feet ahead on the left between houses.

I glanced at the small crack under the hatch, seeing shadows moving and I ran past it, untrusting. I twisted the weight of my shoulder in the last second to ram a slender pale form that charged screaming towards me, clawing with dozens of stacked black talons that echoed all the way down the arm. Pain ignited my bicep as I headed towards the congealing splatter of remains at the end of the street. Above it was a concrete tube which housed the steel rungs of a ladder. My feet slammed the rubber road as I sprinted, and as I ran I felt my lower legs sliced and licked and stung by the pursuing horde right behind me. I ran towards the feeding tube until I was tripped by something shiny and black, the shape of a rhinoceros beetle's horn. I began to fall forward as everything slowed to a crawl.

I aimed my other foot far left to compensate and miraculously didn't topple, continuing to sprint to the encased ladder, which was painted to match the sky mural of the dome wall. Puddles of blood splashed as I ran then jumped, gripping the slick steel rungs tightly to climb as fast as my body would allow. The ladder shaft stank horribly from decades of rot. I felt a deformed wide hand yank me down violently, banging my jaw painfully down on a rung with a stunning blow. I yanked and freed my foot from the boot and the thing let out a high, gurgling scream as it fell. I heard the falling bodies clang against the metal rungs from the tumbling creatures. I used the few seconds of breathing room to push the kitchen knife's blade all the way down between my foot and the inside of my boot. The blade now extended down from under the heel as a makeshift weapon just as the horde returned, angrier.

I felt long fingers wrap around my calf and I stamped violently down, releasing a squeal from the elongated fanged face of that thing below. There were dozens of them, screaming things with too many black orbs of eyes and gnashing jaws. I jammed the blade into a silhouetted head with a downward stomp and climbed faster and higher into the darkness of the tube. Some of the rungs were slippery with blood, and climbing in the darkness became increasingly difficult. I finally reached the top hatch from which that man had been feeding them, and my beating heart sank down into my stomach. It was locked from the other side.

The feedback squeal from the speakers blared, not from above but just below me to the right, repelling the pursuing monstrosities a bit away from me once more as the voice on the system continued. "I'm so sorry, you know I can't let you leave knowing what you know. All our work would be completely destroyed for nothing," followed by another feedback squeal as the speaker cut out. The slobbering, howling sounds of the horde below entered the ladder well once more, echoing demented screams through the narrow space as they closed in. I stepped down a few rungs to the source of the speaker sound and reached over in the blackness and felt a large sliding grate that seemed to be the source of the voice. There was one on my left as well, and neither had locks.

I slid open the grate that led to the speaker's sound and turned on my pocket LED flashlight, placing it pointing inward towards the voice in that duct on the right. I realized the passage might lead to that blind madman on the speaker. I slid the left one open and climbed quickly inside, removing the steak knife from my boot and using it to lift up and close the sliding vent cover behind me. I crawled away slowly and silently in the darkness as I heard scuttling, then screams through the access ladder well that had been repurposed as a food hatch. I listened with a slight feeling of vengeance as that man's screams wailed through the blackness of the space as those things devoured him alive.

Once I'd travelled far enough that I felt confident the light would not be seen, I powered my cell phone on and used it to illuminate the metal passage that seemed to go on forever. I was utterly exhausted, and now finally out of immediate danger, my stomach growled with hunger. When the grate on the end of the ventilation shaft came into view, I exhaled heavily and crawled a bit faster. It was the same sliding kind of the others, and I listened intently, phone screen off to make sure I wasn't seen. Content, I turned it back on, startled by the large face in front of me, a massive painted portrait on the opposite wall.

It was the familiar face of that man who'd left me to die in that suburban shelter, far younger and smiling as he held the test tube, but clearly him. Wood paneling and a groovy rug of swirled hues of blue decorated the space, filled with lava lamps and stereo receivers, speakers and a turntable. His office looked more like a swinger's lounge than an office. I spotted the light switch, flicking it on to see the blacklight lit black velvet paintings of topless women. From the looks of it his office had been untouched for the past forty years. I did love that swanky carpet, but the rest was a bit tacky. I shuffled through papers on his desk, reading a bit before switching off the lights and opening the one wooden door as quietly as possible. I heard saliva-filled, heavy breathing in the dim hallway that door opened to.

There was just one small guidelight in the hall ahead. Glowing orange rings trailed down a hall of elevators. Hope flooded back into my heart as I saw the sign labeled "ground exit". Another hatch, and all I had to do was get by that shadowy shape, scuttling low to the ground with far too many limbs. It was spider-like, two sets of back legs and two sets of arms, elbows and knees pointed upward as it scampered about rapidly in the hall. The head shivered in twitching tics that sent a chill up my spine. An open elevator shaft on the left seemed to answer my question of how it got in here.

I was starving, and headed back to quietly search the lab of Gabe Reverton, the name on the metal plate on his kidney-shaped desk. I rummaged through the drawers and shelves of some stashed rotten foods, finding the savior of a honey jar, which I once read doesn't spoil. I forced down the entire container, licking my fingers and scouring the shelves for more food but finding none. I was going to need my strength if I was going to get past that rapidly moving thing that occupied the elevator bay.

I scanned the room, noticing a standing flag of orange and brown hues with ARK written in a white wave of echoed outlines. I only then realized how much I was bleeding, and ripped the ARK flag from the brass pole, slashing it with scissors from the desk to make bandages to wrap my stinging arm and legs. I stared back nervously at the trail leading to the duct and realized time could be short if those things followed my bloody trail. I picked up the brass flag pole, slapping the heavy metal against my hand, gauging its stopping power.

I searched memos, emergency protocols in the in and out trays of papers on on his desk, reading of elevator reprogramming procedures in case of lockdown, troublesome test results on recent mice and other glimpses into the secret workings of ARK. There were polaroid photos of small, horrifying things in small tanks similar to those I'd seen in larger form, still disturbing in miniature. I found a finances sheet and was amazed at the half million dollar cost of the most basic anti-radiation package offered, which grew after shelter property rental, ration packages, and water, power and heating fees.

This had been a multi-billion dollar facility, with top scientists of the era as well as clientele from around the world. I put together a dossier of the most fascinating papers, including the maps I'd found that showed all of the service, client and employee access entrances and exits. A quick glancing over and I realized I'd be in more risk trying to find another way out at this point. I shoved the paperwork in my pants against my back and tried to mentally ready myself. I removed a blacklight bulb, gripped the flag pole, took a few breaths and slowly opened the door once more, hearing the wet saliva clicking from the spider-like thing's toothy mandibles.

I tossed the long bulb into the elevator shaft, hearing it burst and trickle fragments down deep within. The creature scuttled over in thumping steps, peering over the edge to look within and my heart raced as I seized my chance. I ran and jammed the flagpole into that thing's fleshy side, shoving it into the opening as it squealed a horrific sound. I ran to the ladder and climbed despite the burning in my muscles, higher and higher until I began doubting the shaft would ever end. I heard the squeal behind me then, and it was approaching far too rapidly. As it was nearly upon me, I heard the ambiance thicken and knew I was at the top. I shoved with all my might, expecting it to be locked. It wasn't but it was extremely heavy. I strained and pushed until dirt spilled in and the light of the sky seeped in, I was free.

The moon nearly blinded me as I lay down on the dirt and leaves that covered the thick metal hatch, and to my relief, nothing tried to open it. I caught my breath before searching the dark woods for a small boulder, which I tumbled over to cover that hidden hatch. I turned on my phone's flashlight and breathed deep the fall air, crisp and refreshing after the horrors from below.

I gazed with teary eyes at the moonlit trees, the gradients of Autumn leaves warming the scene with tranquility just above those unimaginable horrors below. I began the long trek back to my car, listening to the peaceful sounds of crickets and bending trees, trying not to think about what I'd read on the paperwork or the horrors still lurking. I was only trying to think of a warm bath and a soft bed, not what I'd seen in those notes. Trying not think about Gabe, Barbara and Calvin, and the three other facilities.

A TERRIFYING WALK AT BODEGA

Author's Note: This is the first "creepypasta" or "nosleep" style story I wrote, trying to make a funny (and intentionally bad) read. Enjoy!

It was near midnight, i remember because I looked at my phone not long before...

I was walking and i suddenly felt a breeze, i remember that because it was a hot night...

I turned the corner and walked into a store to buy gum, and then I noticed the hot dogs...

At first, i just thought they were regular hot dogs, but then I said, "what? why are there hot dogs?"

This particular bodega didn't even SELL hot dogs...

My heart began to flatulate and my eyes got very sweaty, from nervousness. I said "hey there are hot dogs now, but i recant the fact that there were no hot dogs before"

Suddenly my stomach began to hurt and I looked at the man behind the register.

He looked up in the most unforgetable way.

His eyes slowly swivelled upward and then after looking at me he raised his head and said these words.

"I have been selling a hot dogs for over 8 year. it is you who have never been in my store, are you buying a thing"

Sweat was pouring from by eye and I just backed up and left the bodega confused and terrified.

I looked up at the sign and it wasn't a bodega at all, even though I had been on this block for the past 5 months.

This was terrifying enough but as soon as I walked away, I got a text from an unknown sender, and there was a photo of a hot dog, wearing the same outfit as the bodega owner.

To this day I refuse to walk down that street, and sometimes get taxis to drive me out of the way to avoid the street, even though it costs more money.

SPIRALING
DOWN
DISTURBING HORROR STORIES BY
MICHAEL MARKS

"STRIKING, BITING, AND WICKED;
YOU WON'T WANT TO MISS THIS COLLECTION."
PLASTIC
FACES
UNSETTLING STORIES BY
MARTA ABROMAITYTE

STORIES THAT ARE
GUARANTEED TO
ENTERTAIN
VACANCY
R.K. KOMBRINCK
THESE LONELY
PLACES

I'VE DONE
THIS
"TRULY SPECIAL"
BEFORE
A BARRAGE OF
NIGHTMARES BY RYAN MAJOR

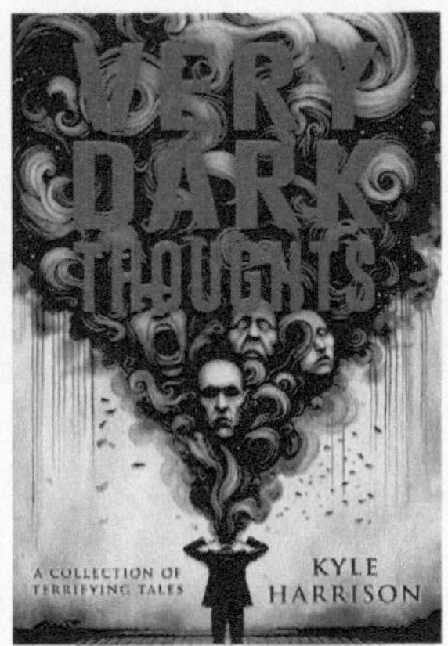
VERY
DARK
THOUGHTS
A COLLECTION OF
TERRIFYING TALES
KYLE
HARRISON

"AN EXCELLENT
COLLECTION
OF HORRORS"
IRON
MAIDENS
TWISTED TALES OF KILLER WOMEN
SARAH JANE HUNTINGTON

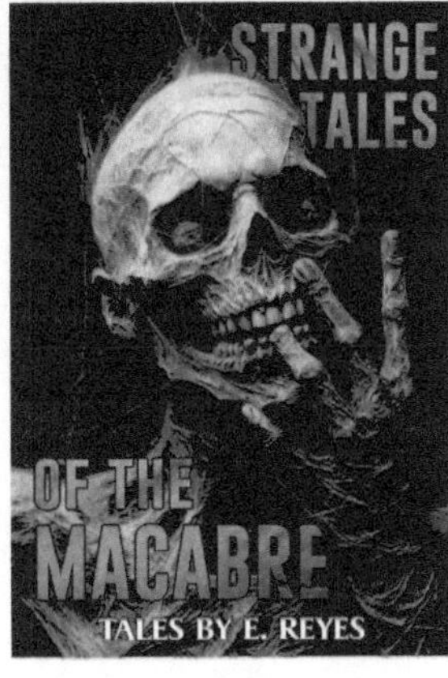
STRANGE
TALES
OF THE
MACABRE
TALES BY E. REYES

FACE DOWN
"A GREAT LITTLE
COLLECTION OF THE
BIZARRE [AND]
MACABRE..."
IN THE
GRAVE
SINISTER TALES BY
THOMAS O.

TRIPPING
"T. W. GRIM CAN
TELL ONE HELL OF
A STORY"
OVER
TWILIGHT
DARK TALES BY
T.W. GRIM

MORE CHILLS FROM VELOX BOOKS

MORE CHILLS FROM VELOX BOOKS